LIGHTNING FORGOTTEN

BY: LILA FELIX

LIGHTNING FORGOTTEN

ISBN:978-1-63422-205-1
Cover Design by: Marya Heiman
Typography by: Courtney Knight
Editing by: Cynthia Shepp

CHAPTER ONE
Theo

THERE WERE SO MANY THINGS GOING WRONG THAT I almost didn't know what was right. Every step and each time we flashed felt like trudging through melted marshmallows, slow and sticky.

All the things we thought were truth were now muddled in a puddle of lies and murky half-honest tales. I was wrong about who I was and what my purpose was. My ego had overridden my heart in telling me that the powers I possessed were only my own.

Yeah, I had an ego. Who knew?

My brother.

Apparently, he knew everything.

Sanctum was a skewed version of me, which was the hardest part for my ego to admit—the fact that he was anything like me pierced me. He had my powers—almost. He had a vast knowledge about this world I'd never dreamed of, and he was running schemes I could never think of if given a lifetime. In some ways, my brother was more powerful than I was, even though most of what he could do was no more than magic tricks in our world.

Dangerous tricks that had the power to kill people and drain them completely of their gifts.

Yet, we were the ones running from him.

We, the ones who had been ordained of the Almighty, were running from him.

Running from him, cowering, pissed me off to no end and made me shrink back in the knowledge that maybe there was a mistake—a big one. The Almighty had chosen the wrong person to carry out His wishes, and there was nothing I could do about it but what we had to do.

On top of everything else, there was the matter of my mate. Colby was living the life I'd always cringed about when I thought about telling her about my powers in the beginning. She was flashing from place to place, desperate to get away from anyone who wanted a piece of what we had so they could take us down. She wasn't flashing because she loved it, because of the thrill it gave her, or the way she embodied light when she used her gift.

I bet she didn't even think of it as a gift anymore—or me.

She was flashing out of a sense of survival. Colby should have never been thrust into this environment of pure survival. It wasn't that she wasn't built for it—she was—but a female like her had never had to experience what we were experiencing now.

I should've left her alone when I had the chance.

She was out of breath, but not from the flashing—from the tremors that life shook her with.

With a hand placed against her chest, she said, "I think we lost him for a bit. Or at least for a minute. Maybe even the devil's dealer needs sleep too." She dusted the sands of Saudi Arabia from the bottom of her white dress with a grimace. I'd always groaned at Colby's high-maintenance attitude, but in times like these, I wished for one second that she'd have the luxury to be like that again.

I'd bring her to whatever store she wanted in a heartbeat, buy her everything.

I looked in all directions. At this point, I wouldn't be surprised if Sanctum popped up from one of the enormous mounds of sand and roared like that mummy guy from the movie. "I don't know. It seems like every time we think we're ahead of them, we're, in fact, just a few steps behind," I said, running a thumb over the top of her cheek to remove some of the desert particles before they got in her eye.

The problem we were facing was not unique. It was a time-tested problem that every race and species went through. The struggle for power was one that would never be overcome, no matter how long the world turned. My brother was not exempt. I knew the truth about what he was now. He was just another power-hungry individual who allowed it to go to his head, even though he claimed to be just a minion for the one who really wanted dominion.

I didn't believe him for one second. That man I once knew as Torrent had the devil in his eyes.

When she bit her lip, I knew she was thinking. "At this point, I don't even care. I just don't give a damn about it right now. I'm exhausted. I need some sleep—even if it's in a tent with goats or whatever animal they have around here. Are there camels? I freakin' love camels." She turned in a circle to survey the area, realization dawning on her face that there were no tents or even goats around to keep her company for a bit of sleep. There was only sand and wind, with wind blowing the sand and sand blowing in the wind.

Her smartass comments were at an all-time high today.

Somehow, they multiplied with her level of stress.

She hated camels.

"I'm sorry," I breathed, scooping her up into my arms so that at least her feet might find some rest. We landed in several places, some of which weren't the smooth, slick marble that her feet were used to padding on. We'd gone to her favorite tunnel in Tokyo. She'd cut one of her

4

toes on the corroded middle of the rails, and she'd nicked her arm on one of the mountains in the Appalachians. And when we landed in South America, I had to catch her before she fell directly into a volcano. Apparently, we'd come across an older Google map.

It felt like she weighed a little less, but it was nothing to worry about. We'd both missed a couple of meals here and there.

"It's okay." She struggled and wriggled until I could hold on no more. My resolve had faltered as the time went by about when I would be able to get back into the Fray. This was how weak I had become—how weak I was in general. I couldn't even keep hold of Colby when she needed me most. I found that while the Fray no longer drained me completely of my energy as I traveled between our world and there, that the longer I stayed away, the frailer I got. I contributed it to the number of souls that were still getting stuck there. The numbers were increasing as we gave the powers back to our Lucent brothers and sisters who had been stripped of them so mercilessly.

Someone needed to teach them the rules— as much as I hated them. It was like we needed to put out a pamphlet titled 'You Got Your Powers Back. Now What?'.

In the meantime, there was nothing I could do to help the situation. I feared that one day, Colby would turn around, look me straight in the eye like she did the night of her eighteenth birthday, and tell me it was over.

She should've done it a while ago.

"It's not okay. I'm failing again. I know how much I try to balance all of this, but then something falls astray and there's not a damn thing I can do about it."

I hated this part of me that had come to fruition as I came into my powers and recognized them for what they were—a blessing and a curse. They were a blessing in that I could help our species to become who they needed to be regardless of the powers that stood against us. It was a curse that my mate, Colby, would always be the person who fell to the wayside as I strived to do the best I could to save people. As much as I loved giving the people back their powers, when it was done, there was nothing more I wanted than to give my gifts back to the one who gave them to me in the first place. I wished sometimes that Sanctum would strip me of my powers, leaving me to only one duty—to Colby.

Winking at me, she tried to make light of the situation. She tended to do that lately, but it seemed insincere when it wasn't laced with sarcasm. She was either too much of a smartass or over-the-top nice.

"Hey, hey, we don't have time for that. There will be time for wallowing in the regret soon enough, but today is not that day." She was quoting Aragorn, and I loved her for it. I certainly felt like we were in the last battle.

All this time, I thought I would be the stronger of the two in our coupling because of my gift. But as she grew more in strength and knowledge about who she was and what the Almighty had put her on this earth for, I knew that, as with all Lucent men, I was the weaker of the two of us.

I would always be weaker than her—most of the time, I didn't mind.

And the fact that she recognized my wallowing in self-pity just made it all the worse. It was funny that when I was ordinary, I wished for more. I wished to give her a normal life—at least as normal as a Lucent life could be. We could be together, traveling the world and maybe even the universe for the rest of eternity together. But now that I had it in my hands— this power that was once only reserved for the females of the listed species—all I wanted to do was give it back.

"You know what's crazy?" she asked, taking my hand and pulling me in a direction that neither of us was certain where it would lead.

"No." I was too exhausted to even conjure up any sarcasm for her at this point. There was sand on my tongue and my lips were wind chapped from the constant hot air coming off the desert floor.

"I'm not feeling him anymore..." She paused,

her steps halting in the sand while still holding my hand as tightly as possible. "At all. I can't pinpoint his location."

"I don't know if that's better or not." I thought about it for an instant, finding I was relieved not to have him with me anymore. He was like a tick buried deep in my skin. I knew exactly where he was, but, for the life of me, I couldn't remove him. But then the thought of not knowing his location scared me more than knowing where he was at every moment.

"Let's not think about it right now. The only thing I want to think about is a place to sleep and water on my tongue," she said, practically dragging me over a mountain that never seemed to end, yet when I looked back, it never seemed to begin.

Her hair blew in all directions and it reminded me of why I loved her once again.

Even though she'd changed, that part of Colby showed itself once in a while. It was the part that was unruly. It was the piece that remained of the teenager who would do anything for what she wanted. She was wild and impractical. She wanted what she wanted, when she wanted it, no matter the cost or how it came to be. Every once in a while, that beautiful girl would show herself to me once again. However, she was nothing compared to the woman, the female in front of me who had somehow agreed to be my mate for the rest of eternity.

"Where's the Viking? Where are the others?" she said more to herself than to me. Another thing that had changed about Colby was that she was constantly concerned about the welfare of others. She could be trusted, just as she wholly believed in those who she now called her confidantes and friends. It was those few people we could depend on above all others.

"Collin is in California," I said, coughing with my hand over my eyes to shield them from the ever-blowing sand. "He's on the beach near Los Angeles. Probably Venice or Santa Monica. I'm all foggy. That's the best I can do. Everything is starting to meld together."

The Viking was probably bug-eyed at the barely there bikinis and California girls. He was probably advising them to cover up. Ari tried to wear a shirt that was open in the back one time, and he ripped the tablecloth from the dining room table and covered her up. She looked like a lazy kid who had dressed up like a ghost for Halloween.

Colby stopped and sighed. She did a lot of that lately.

"You've been gone too long. It's been weeks. You forget that I can now feel the longing. I know that it's not your personal longing, but the guilt that keeps you here with me and yet calls to you from the place where you are needed."

I changed my mind. That was the worst part. Since we've bonded, she now knew when I was longing to be in the place that my mind didn't really want to be. She knew—connected with me like our souls were smaller pieces of one.

"It's okay. I won't leave you unprotected from Sanctum and the Synod. It's not that bad anyway."

There was a time when her snark would've cut me wide open, but now was not the time. She knew it felt like the Fray was ripping my chest out through my skin since I couldn't be helping people in that place where souls were aimlessly wandering.

Instead, I was running from my idiot, once-upon-a-time brother.

"Do they all want to get to Paraiso?" she asked.

I stopped dead in my tracks. What was she thinking? Of course they all wanted to go to Paraiso—where else would they go?

My voice was clipped as I answered, "They certainly don't want to stay in the Fray for eternity"

Her jaw moved as she chewed on the inside of her mouth. "But some of them are children, right? What if they just want to be returned to their families? I know the ones you brought across before had been there so long that their loved ones had moved on, but what about the new ones? Maybe they just want to go home. Maybe…"

"What?" I was so stupid.

"Nothing. I just thought maybe—I wish we knew how Torrent came to be Sanctum."

A needling of anger went through me. Colby and I had still not discussed the events that occurred the first time I was in the Fray. I knew from Collin that Sanctum and Colby had gone off together, apparently planning the murder of the Synod, but beyond that, we had been a little too busy to talk about it.

"Why? What does that have to do with the Fray?"

She shrugged. "Nothing. I was just wondering. Knowing what happened to him might give us some insight—if those without powers can be given them back—Torrent can be good again."

She didn't understand. Since this restoration of powers to people had started, she thought everyone could be restored. The thing was—some people were too far gone for it to work.

Even my brother.

CHAPTER TWO
Colby

I THOUGHT WHEN THE ALMIGHTY APPROVED OF THEO and my joining with the lightning wrapping around our hands, that somehow, I'd gotten a little more than I was supposed to.

I also, deep down inside, assumed that the rest of whatever our journey held would be easy. Turned out, I was flat wrong.

It seemed like every day I got a little more insight into certain things, but the path for us and the path for our race couldn't be cloudier.

More and more, I could physically feel where Lucents were—not just locating people I knew, but knowing where all of them were at the same time. But I wasn't ready to tell Theo yet. He had enough.

He was pissed about me even asking about Sanctum. I knew that the time I'd spent planning a murder plot that would never come to fruition hadn't sat well with him. Regardless of the fact that I didn't even have the stomach to kill. It was another subject that had been put on the back burner. The other one was the fact that Pema was missing and had been for some time.

And the little thing where my dead grandmother whispered to me from the beyond that his brother had slit her throat open.

Just little things like that.

"Let's just find somewhere to stay for the night, and then we can get into all the things we want to discuss. My brain can't function with this much sand around. It's not like beach sand that makes you relax just at the sight. This kind makes me stressed out." It was a lie, of course. She loved sand in any form, from beaches to deserts. When we stopped, all we did was sleep and shove food into our mouths. I pretended to eat, but it seemed like anything I attempted to eat either came back up or refused to go down in the first place.

Another issue no one had the time to pursue.

I nodded and said, "There should be a place up ahead."

I didn't know if it was a place, per se, but it was definitely a grouping of Lucents. Hopefully they knew who Theo was—it would be the one time that his Eidolon title would be gladly thrown around, though he and I would feel wretched using it for our own selfish purpose.

I'd become a name-dropper.

He hadn't noticed that I knew exactly where to go while we were running—he didn't have the space to—the Fray called to him and nothing else mattered.

The thing was—that was part of why I loved him—his devotion to our people.

I'd once thought it was his blind devotion to me that kept me head over heels, but the opposite was true. His love for me was unwavering, which was why my ego had been mostly shut down after our sealing was complete. There was no need for ego in a coupling like ours—no need at all.

We'd probably walked for hours before spotting a grouping of tents. I could feel the warmth of my people like a lone star in the darkness.

I nodded in the direction of the tents. The smell of food and the glow from a light beckoned me. "There. Finally."

Theo stepped in front of me. "Let me go check it out. What if it's not safe?"

I kissed the back of his neck. "Then we'll protect each other."

A man with the longest beard I'd ever seen emerged from the tent before we reached the door, startling me. When I got a hold of my heartbeat, I smiled. I was glad he came out because it wasn't possible to knock on the door of a tent. If he hadn't come out, I would've resorted to whistling.

That wasn't the wisest thing, probably.

The Almighty knew that manners weren't really my strong suit.

"Welcome to our humble home. We've been waiting for you." The man, more belly than brawn, opened his arms wide and motioned into the tent. He wore a long, robe-like outfit with bright, rich colors. His smile was genuine and inviting.

"You've been waiting for us?" Theo questioned. He took nothing at face value, but with what had happened to us lately, I didn't blame him one bit.

The tent flap opened, revealing a woman twice as beautiful as any female I'd ever seen. Her black hair blew in the desert wind. She looked like she was made of olive oil and cardamom. I could hear laughter and conversation coming from inside.

The man pointed to the woman and pulled her under his arm. "This is my daughter, Malynn. She is clairvoyant. She's seen the Eidolon's coming for years. But some things are better kept to one's self—but I'm sure you two know that. Please, come inside and make yourselves at home. We are honored to have you."

If that wasn't a welcome, I didn't know what was.

And no, I had no idea what the hell he was talking about.

When I walked into the tent, I realized it wasn't a tent at all—more like a portable mansion of magic and luxury.

In other words—it was my kind of place.

"My son, Kareem." He flicked his wrist to a male version of Malynn. "He manifests mirages, which is convenient in the desert. Our tents are hidden from everyone who might seek us for harm. To anyone else, our tent would appear as a group of palm trees. But to you or other Lucent, it appears as what it is, a haven."

Not even five minutes in and these people were showing off. I was a little relieved not to be the only one in the room with superpowers.

But I still didn't really know who they were or how they knew who we were.

Theo cleared his throat. "Who are you? What is your name, sir?"

The Eidolon still said 'sir' to people. He would never change.

"Omar. My name is Omar. Eidolon, we are here to keep you safe, you and your mate. You are too young to remember us, aren't you? We are the Clandestine."

I knew who these people were, but I had to wrack my brain for a few minutes to recall their purpose. My fingers pressed against my temple, trying to force the neurons to do my bidding. They were only mentioned here or there like a species that had gone extinct without anyone's knowledge.

"The keepers? No, wait, that's close, right?" Theo was guessing too. Even with all the history I knew about our people, I didn't know

16

enough—I might not ever know enough.

"We are not keepers of anything, Eidolon. We are protectors and servants of the Eidolon and his family—but we can only protect if the Eidolon seeks us. I believe that's why you are here. It is not an accident that you were guided here. There is a purpose to all of us being together. Now enough business. Let's eat, drink, and celebrate. Long have we waited to perform our duty once more."

I was leaning more and more on Theo's gift of discernment when it came to people. He'd never trusted Sanctum like I had. I'd never trusted Collin in the beginning, and he turned out to be my most-valued companion.

I overthought everything.

Even this.

But when Theo smiled at Omar and accepted the invitation, I knew it was okay.

"Come on, mate. We are safe here." Theo grabbed my hand and pulled me down to sit on a spread of lavish carpets beside a low table filled with food I had never before eaten, but that looked delicious.

"Please, Eidolon, Queen, eat. There is no place safer than with us."

Um, did that dude just call me queen?

More lanterns and candles were lit. After they were, the real breadth of the tent was revealed. It was at least twenty times bigger than it appeared from the outside, and there were more people in it than I could count. Families and children talked and played together.

"You're all Clandestine?" I stuttered, still in awe.

"Yes. All of us. Truly, there is nothing to fear here." Omar's smile reassured me, but only a little.

I wasn't scared, yet I was still skeptical. Again, I looked to Theo.

"It's okay, Querida. You found this place. Let yourself rest."

I didn't know if it was the soothing tone my love was speaking to me in or the fact that the tent was so warm and inviting, but my lips never touched food or drink that night. And I didn't get to say all the things I wanted to. There were no questions asked.

I slumped against Theo's shoulder and passed out cold.

CHAPTER THREE

Theo

COLBY WOULD BE THE LAST TO ADMIT HOW TIRED SHE was, but everyone around us knew. The words were hardly out of my mouth before she was asleep.

Omar stood. "Come, we have a place to sleep ready for you."

The surprise must've showed on my face.

He smiled at me. It reminded me of my father's. "We have waited a long time, but we never lost hope."

I was glad they hadn't. I'd lost hope a long time ago.

"Show me the way." I gathered her up and followed Omar to a bedroom of sorts near the front of the tent. Royal blue, magenta, and gold fabric decorated the ceiling of the room and flowed down to the floor, which held a bed more comfortable looking than the one I had in my childhood home. The soft glow of candles filled the space and the lullaby scent of lavender wafted from incense on the small table, the only furniture in the room.

"Leave her to rest. We have much to talk about. My daughter has many questions."

As we left, a woman, about the same age as Malynn took station outside Colby's room. She reminded me of a Secret Service agent, except prettier and less—stiff. After following Omar back and talking to his daughter, I found that he was correct and Malynn wasn't shy about anything she wanted to know. She asked questions, pointed ones, but some of them were vague. While I trusted them on the surface, I was still apprehensive. After all, I'd made many mistakes before about who could and could not be trusted. I tested her first, of course, though my instincts said that these people were legit.

"I saw the demon. It woke me from a sleep like the mummies." Her English wasn't all that good.

I tried not to laugh. "Like the dead. It woke you from a sleep like the dead. What demon?" I knew exactly which demon she referred to, but, again, I wasn't giving too much away too soon.

She drew her hands up over her head and bent her fingers into deadly claws. "Like this and his foul breath made you..." She showed me shivering. It was like playing the Lucent version of charades.

"It made me shudder, yes. Someone brought him to where he belongs."

She flexed her fingers, almost reaching into space for more information. "The brother—the brother brought him to hell. He was rewarded." Her voice grew coarse like some of the desert sand had gotten trapped in her throat.

It struck my core the way she still called him my brother. In my heart, he was no family of mine. Everyone still called him my brother—even Colby. Collin and Ari were closer to being my family than that bastard would ever be again. But I played along. "Who was rewarded?"

"Sanctum." She whispered the word, but it was for naught. The rest of our company gasped at the calling of such evil. One woman covered her daughter's ears as if Malynn had uttered a curse word. "He was given the right to have a child—a privilege once taken from him in return for his gifts. That was his reward."

I reached up in frustration and fisted the roots of my hair. Just when I thought I'd figured something out, it all came unwound.

Who would ever give my brother the gift of having offspring?

A little Damion Lucent running around was all the world needed.

Malynn turned and had a heated conversation. They were speaking so fast that even if I spoke the language, I probably would've been lost. Strained tones and harsh syllables met each other in a small battle.

"What is it?" I asked, wanting in on whatever

was wrong.

Malynn wrung her hands. "Did I say something wrong? He is your brother, correct? I don't understand." She turned around and more strong, pointy words and aggressive voices were thrown around.

I held up my palm as if for them to stop arguing. "It's not you. You didn't say anything wrong. I know none of this. Everything you're saying is news to me. I mean, I know he is— was—my brother, but other than that, I am in the dark."

Malynn took a long sip of her tea while the rest of the group went back to their previous conversation as if nothing had happened. "I didn't know. We assumed you knew such things. It's fine. Should we start at the beginning then?"

And start at the beginning, we did—at the beginning of time. I had only thought Colby knew her history. This woman spoke as if she were there from the beginning, like Eve was her bestie.

"Your brother wasn't born into his role. Don't let him joke you into believing that." The word was trick, but I didn't have the energy to start correcting her. "At some point, he summoned the evil one, the devil, Satan, the adversary, the name doesn't matter. Your brother asked for his place. He asked to be the one to destroy the Eidolon. I don't know if this was before or after he knew it was you. You'll have to ask him that yourself. In exchange for his place, he gave up his soul. It is on lean? Is that how you say it? Lean?"

"Lease? My brother's soul is on lease?" He'd treated his soul like a car trade-in.

She snapped and smiled. "Yes, so what he's doing is paying rent of sort. He earns more time with his soul and in life by doing wrong."

I let some of that settle along with my food, which was already threatening to upheave after less than three bites. Every time my brother did something wrong, he gained more time in this life—more time to do more horrible things.

"What about—you said something about a child."

Malynn reached behind her neck, pulling her hair around and resting the length across her lap. It flowed around her like a thick, black snake. "You had the power to kill that demon in the Fray, but instead, you brought Sanctum there and he transported the demon to hell. It was like returning a soldier to the enemy's army. He was rewarded with something he was missing—he chose to regain the power to have a child. That was taken from him when he took the job as your villain. I believe he took many demons back to their maker. A child was his reward for the first one, but that is the only reward he will ever get, no matter how many he brings back."

She meant nemesis, but I nodded anyway.

"What else? What else did he give to be so evil? Why would he choose it?"

She poured herself another cup of tea and sprinkled in some kind of star-shaped spice that smelled like licorice when heated.

"If he knew who or what you were—then it was personal. If not, I don't know what his motives were. And he gave everything to have the powers he does. His life, his soul, but mostly, he gave up love. He is unable to love or receive love. At least, that's the way we understand it."

So either my brother hated me all the way back to when I still thought he carved the craters in the moon, or else, he was already evil and sought to enhance it.

No matter which way I looked at it, none of it made sense.

Torrent was raised the same as me. There was no favoritism or golden child in our family. We had the same opportunities and parents. I couldn't even begin to imagine a reason why he would choose the path he did.

I breathed out an emotion-filled sigh. Giving me this information was like adding another layer of books to a pile that I would never have time to read. "At least we know he doesn't have a child. Maybe we can stop him before he procreates."

The only sound I heard in response was the wind and the gentle flapping of the tent's edges. Malynn looked down into her teacup.

"What? He's been with me the whole time. Well, not the whole time." He would have had to cultivate a relationship with someone to have a child with them. At least, that was the way it should've been. If someone was going to have the child of the nastiest being I knew, then at least they could be friends first.

Omar chuckled from the back, showing me a small measure with his forefinger and thumb. "It only takes a little bit of time." The men huddled around him laughed at the dig.

"There's a child?" I whispered the question into the night.

Malynn looked behind me, over my shoulder. "Colby, please join us. We have no secrets here."

I turned around as Colby came out of the shadows. If possible, she looked worse for the wear. Her hair had been brushed and wrapped into a braid. "You know what's strange?" my mate mumbled. "Without all the noise—this place is so quiet. Is it weird that I couldn't sleep without all the noise around us?"

"It's the same when we go to the city for small periods of time. I can't stand the noise," Malynn answered, motioning for Colby to sit down. She made Colby a similar cup of tea to hers and pushed it in her direction. "This will make you feel better."

If anything, it looked like the sight of the brewing liquid was making her worse by the second. "Thank you."

I waited a moment for the answer to my question. It wasn't that hard. If my brother—Sanctum—was going to be a father, then ending him, the plan in my mind, was no longer an option. And I hated to admit it, but Colby's earlier mention of fixing him, well, we might have to explore that.

Even though I hated him, I wouldn't take a father away from their child—no matter how vile.

I hated being such a softie.

In my mind, I wanted to kill them all, the Synod, my brother, all of them who stood against us. But it just wasn't in me to carry out a massacre when I wasn't even armed for such a fight.

Colby took a few sips and her eyebrow popped up, a sure sign that she liked it. "So, you were saying something about Sanctum and a child? Who would—I mean, who would agree to have his child? Ewww."

Her eww was met with laughter. "I can't see her face for some reason. She is clouded. I believe he has some kind of protection around her for this very purpose. He must know about us—or is concerned that someone would seek to end her if they knew. The babe grows in her stomach, only weeks old, maybe a few months. But there's another issue."

Of course there was. There was always another issue with these people—with our people—all of it.

"What's the issue?" My voice was laced with frustration and rightfully so.

"He thinks the child is his, which is why he protects the mother." She looked saddened, and a tear welled in one of her eyes. I couldn't imagine what would make Malynn have any kind of sympathy for my brother. He was the enemy. "When one makes the contract to become Sanctum—nothing belongs to them anymore. He was allowed to have a child, but it belongs to Sanctum's master. When you work for the devil, even your thoughts belong to him."

CHAPTER FOUR
Sanctum

"Quit your whining. We don't have a choice. You agreed to this, remember?" The female wasn't even through her first trimester, and her whining was making me want to slit my own throat.

I was good at slitting throats; Rebekkah knew that before she faded away.

She paced in the miniscule cabin from corner to corner like a caged tiger. She could do that until she was blue in the face, but I wasn't letting her out of here unless I had to. I couldn't take a chance on her leaving. He would take her—I knew he would. He thought I was stupid. I knew that granting me permission to have a child would not be without strings. Everything had strings with His Evilness.

If he found her—he'd never let me have this one piece. It was the last shred of humanity I might ever get, and it was sitting in the stomach of the most annoying female I'd ever known.

Yeah, regret was a big word in my vocabulary now. It was all I thought about—all that plagued me.

Pema's little voice interrupted my self-degradation. "I agreed because I thought you might love me if I carried your child."

She had the most backward thinking of them all. In the beginning, she had been desperate for anyone's attention. And the more she clung to me, the more I thought there might be a chance that she would carry the child. Having a descendant of the previous Eidolon carrying the love child of Sanctum was my own private entertainment.

I snapped my fingers at her. She gasped and put both hands over her stomach, but I wasn't falling for the fake drama. "Look at me, Pema. I'm not capable of flowers and chocolate. I'm capable of death, destruction, and ruining the lives of Lucents. That's my deal. It's not like you thought you were going to carry the baby of an archangel."

My voice didn't sound half as badass as I wanted it to.

Her begging became whimpers. "I'll be careful. I can still travel. It won't hurt the baby."

I waved her off. I was simply taunting her, of course. If she kept it up, I would chain her skinny legs to the bed. There was nothing I wouldn't do to save the child. Having a child meant saving a tiny piece of me.

I turned to the small rectangle of a window and opened the shutters. "Fine. Go. But if he catches you and brings you down to hell, I won't come get you."

She and I both knew it was a lie. I'd become fond of the little brat from day one. But unfortunately for her, fondness was all I was capable of. It was the kind of affection I felt for anyone who could help me on my way to whatever I wanted—simple and shallow. At one point, I'd felt the same way about the Synod until they actually grew a conscious and stopped doing my bidding.

What Pema didn't know was that there was no reason to get attached to the fetus. Even she should think of the damned thing for exactly what it was—a thing. I'd already decided. It would go to Colby and Theo to raise—maybe the spawn would grow up good and be some kind of redemption in my memory.

That was, if I let Theo live—or Colby for that matter.

Or maybe he would be like me—a prick so consumed with jealousy over his brother that he damned himself for eternity. Wouldn't that be fitting?

If I could go back to that day—so long ago—I would do it in a heartbeat. There was nothing else I wanted more. The things a kid thought were so damned important actually weren't. They were just big because I was so little.

I heard her sigh and knew that another complaint was coming. "I hate this thing around my neck. It creeps me out."

I rolled my eyes at having to explain myself again. "It's just a necklace. It keeps everyone from finding you."

It was so much more than a necklace. It held the key to how I would eventually make Theo do anything I wanted him to—maybe some things I hadn't even planned on. It was all too easy to link the two together—that which he loved to no end and that which I wanted to no end.

Colby was so stupid to have trusted me in the first place—Colby and Pema—ignorant females who believed every word that came off my tongue.

But that was why I needed Theo and Colby, both of them, to raise the little brat—so it wouldn't grow up to be me.

Speaking of Theo, I reached into my psyche and felt around for the little twit. I'd quit chasing them about a week ago, but they'd kept running like morons. I'd always been one step behind.

Not a lot had changed since we were kids— still pulling the caboose of life.

Gripping the wall next to me, I groaned and strained against the walls of my mind.

"What? What's happened?" the pixie asked. I needed to find her some more things to entertain her. Maybe she could copy a dictionary or something. Anything to stop her consistent questioning.

Inside my mind, I searched for Theo and Colby but came up empty.

"I can't feel them—at all. No, not at all. He said I'd know when Theo was dead—like a part of me had died as well. I didn't feel anything, so why in the hell can't I pinpoint him? I can't find him!"

Pema's eyes were wide as saucers, so I calmed myself on the outside while I was livid on the inside.

Couldn't upset the incubator too much. She was carrying my one shot.

"I'm going to the Synod. They have to help me. I'll slaughter them all if they don't."

CHAPTER FIVE
Colby

"HOW LONG CAN WE STAY HERE, THEO?" I WHISPERED TO him in the dark. He wasn't asleep. I could tell by his breathing that he was stewing. He hadn't moved an inch since lying down. He was on his back, coffin style, and I knew that wasn't his usual routine.

After a few seconds, he finally answered me. "I don't know. Long enough to get things figured out, but not so long that he starts doing something in retribution. We've come so far—I'd hate for him to start killing people."

I snorted. "He can take it out on Regina all he wants to. She'd probably enjoy it."

"I think it's the other way around, Querida. She likes to see people suffer."

I sat up straight, and my breath hitched in my throat. "Wait. What if we confused everyone?"

Theo chuckled and turned over to face me. "We already do confuse everyone. Well, mostly you do. What do you mean?"

He got popped on the hip for that one.

"I mean, what if we convinced The Synod

that Sanctum was after them and we had to band together to take Sanctum out? I don't think they are really talking as he's been too busy chasing us and—and getting busy."

A shudder took over me just saying the words. But I was desperate—desperate to be rid of Sanctum and to have a simpler life.

Theo chuckled and sat behind me, trying to wrap me in a hold, but I wriggled free. "An enemy of our enemy is our friend. But you forgot one thing. The Synod hates you—a lot."

I had been thinking about that at length as we traveled. Yes, the Synod had always been snotty to me, but I'd been twice or three times as snotty right back to them.

I went into the first meeting with a chip on my shoulder the size of Idaho.

Going back, I knew it was because of Rebekkah that I felt that way. They'd undermined my grandmother by stripping her of her official title and telling everyone that the prophets weren't to be trusted anymore.

I knew from the time I was small that they were a necessary enemy. We had to get along with them, but we didn't have to like it.

They deserved all of it. Right?

Rebekkah told me to rethink everything I thought was truth—she didn't discriminate which truth and how much I should look beyond it.

I looked around our surroundings, still not

believing we were safe. Somehow, it was easier to believe that it was temporary—that any moment we would have to run again—than to believe we really were hidden as Omar claimed. "We all deserve a second chance, right? Maybe they will listen to me. Maybe for once in my life they will take me seriously."

Theo shot up next to me. "You're not going in there alone. Don't even think about it. We've been through this."

There was no way to tell him that I'd already made up my mind and he needed to respect my decision, putting all of his machismo to the side.

Not that he had very much in him—most of it was just regular old boy protecting girl instincts.

If we were regular people, it would be cute.

But I'd never been the cutesy type.

There wasn't even a point in discussing the issue or wasting our time arguing over something that *would* happen.

After kissing the side of his neck in a sad attempt at distracting him, I folded. "I'll take Collin with me. We have to try, and you're way too emotional about everything. Plus, they need to think you're in the Fray, doing what you have to."

It didn't take long to convince him.

His shoulders slumped. "When?"

"I was planning on going to get Collin tonight.

He's still in California. Malynn said it was okay. She's seen him in a vision or whatever she has."

Theo's eyes darted around the room, back to me, and then did the dance again. "Take one of the Clandestine—even two of them—with you. I won't risk your life again. If you insist on doing this alone, then at least take them."

"I'll take one, along with Collin," I answered as dryly as I could. I knew that I'd won, but it didn't feel anything like winning. It felt like I'd manipulated him.

Theo lay down sideways and rested his head on my thighs. His hair was longer than he usually let it grow, but haircuts weren't exactly at the top of our list of things to get done. I combed my fingers through the raven strands, loving how after only two or three strokes, he was almost asleep.

"How did it come to this?" he said. His eyes were closed and I felt the heat of his breath through my thin dress. It was a serious moment, but I couldn't take it anymore. It had been weeks since I saw Theo smile. If my smartass comments couldn't do it, then we'd never get through this unscathed—well, any more than we already were.

I had to resort to his kind of humor. I was actually surprised at how good I was getting at it.

"Really? I'm trying to be serious and you're quoting the *Return of the King*? You've got to be kidding me. I bet you're planning to binge on those DVDs the next time you have free time, aren't you? Don't think just because we are sealed now that you can make me watch them either. I said one time, and I meant it. And I saw you searching for elven ears on eBay one time. I'm not going to participate in some weird *Lord of the Rings* dress-up game with you."

He was cracking. The redness at the tips of his ears told me that a few more quips like that and he was mine for the taking—smile wise.

"And don't think I don't remember that you haven't seen those prequel dragon movies either. I saw you reading *The Hobbit* when we were kids. It wasn't even the cool version either. It was the pathetic paperback with the fat, cartoon hobbit on the front. I wanted to throw it in the ditch and buy you a new one. Wait… you watched the cartoon version too, didn't you? I bet Peter Jackson watched it too."

By the time I finished my spiel, he was done for. His smile had turned to a laugh so intense that his arms were wrapped around his middle, helping him stay together.

"You know," he said, after he'd gotten a hold of himself. "You say you hate those movies, but you know the director and everything about them, including when I'm quoting them. And you've been quoting them too. I think you watch them in secret, and you know what else?"

He sprang up to a sitting position, grabbed me around the waist, and hoisted me onto his lap. "I think you love them because I love them and you love anything I love. Because inside, you're a big softie and…" He moved to whisper in my ear. "A little bit nerdy, meu amor."

Now he'd gone too far—way too far.

I had so many arguments in my mouth, right on the tip of my tongue, but they were all trapped by a gasp at the sensation of Theo's tongue at the side of my neck. He knew exactly how to drive me mad and how to shut me up.

I was pathetic, and he was magic.

"You're so tense." He pulled back and waited until we'd made eye contact, which I avoided, still stewing about the nerd comment. "Querida, we are here, in this beautiful home, made of silk and linen. We are protected by ancient soldiers who were born and bred for our protection and safety. Can't you give in a little?"

I could give in a lot.

I wrapped my legs around his hips and drew him closer, reveling in his scent and the way he held me. His mouth moved to my ear. I drew in a deep breath as his teeth grazed my earlobe. Ever since the lightning had sealed us together, it sent sparks through both of us whenever we were this intimate. I could hear the crackles and snaps of it as it ran from his body to mine.

It connected us in a way that nothing else in the world possibly could.

CHAPTER SIX
Collin

I'D NEVER WORN SUNGLASSES IN MY LIFE UNTIL COMING to California. But the blaring sun and the reflection of it off the ocean's surface made me seek eye protection on my first day. There was a stand right on Venice beach, near a man who wore roller skates while he played an electric guitar, which sold the less obscure ones. I picked out a black pair and then sent Ari a picture—she called them selfies—of me with my ridiculous cell phone. I'd had the phone for years, but it was simply something that was kept in my pocket in case the Synod needed to contact me outside of my home.

She approved and insisted I pick her out a pair.

Sitting on the edge of the sidewalk that separated the Venice walkway from the sands of the beach, I watched as the sun bathed the people in its warmth. There was so much to do in this crevice of Los Angeles, but I wanted to stay in one place in case Theo or Colby needed me. They wouldn't have trouble finding me if I stayed still until further notice.

I missed my home. To the outside world, it was a stiff, staunch library, filled with decaying artifacts and whittled-away paper documents. Not even the members of the Synod would visit, and it was their books under my care. But to me, it was the only place I'd ever belonged. I was brought there at the tender age of twelve. The Guardian before me taught me how to take care of the books and how to protect them and myself. I never questioned the station or my job—it was what I was born for and I'd always considered it a privilege.

I did, however, notice strange things a little after my thirteenth birthday. As the people played volleyball and sunbathed before me, all I could do was roll those events through my head. Every once in a while, the Synod would call and request certain documents to be shipped to them so they could electronically transfer them. When they returned, they were missing pages and, in some cases, missing entire chapters. When I asked Devrin, the Guardian in charge, he simply told me not to speak of it—that doing so would anger the Synod.

That was when I learned that nothing was as it seemed—especially the Synod.

But I said nothing—as we were taught. Stupid guardians that we were, we never questioned the orders.

Shortly after, I began to keep records of the mishaps in secret. I had leather-bound journals of every size and fashion hidden within the walls of my room until, at eighteen, the Guardianship was officially passed to me.

My home was then my own to keep.

I kept them everywhere in the library, camouflaged as Lucent texts.

Until Theodore showed up, at least.

I knew the first time he muttered the word Eidolon that my life would never be the same.

I burned all the journals the night after he left—every single one of them. I needed to be blemish-less in the eyes of the Synod for the Eidolon. Because he would have few witnesses in the beginning, and I would be one of them.

As I thought about all we'd gone through, a text message came through from Colby. I hadn't heard from them in days and truly hadn't expected to. They didn't worry about the people around them because they knew where they were just by thinking about them, but the rest of us worried about our not-so-fearless leaders.

I'm coming to get you. Get somewhere private.

I shook my head when I read the message. She sent a little picture of a blushing face. There were always innuendos with that girl.

They never stopped.

Give me ten minutes.

Ten minutes is all I get?

Innuendos.

I replied quickly and then darted back to my hotel room. It was a cheap place with no security cameras to speak of, so there would be no evidence if Colby decided to poof in public.

That was how long I'd been around Ari and Colby—I'd been deduced to using their language. The Synod would curl their toes if they heard anyone refer to flashing as poofing.

But it made Ari giggle, so there was that.

I made sure to stay in a place that was less secure, and, by default, less sanitary. I hoped she was bringing me to some place with a shower at the least.

I was afraid of the one in our room, and I wasn't afraid of much.

I had kept my bag packed for such an occasion and grabbed it, standing there like someone waiting on a train—the Colby Express.

When she arrived, there was hardly any wake at all—a flickering of a lightbulb to the untrained eye. She'd been traveling so frequently that her lightning wasn't lightning at all anymore.

"Your wake is tired. Just like you are," I said before thinking. The last thing she needed was someone reminding her of the obvious.

"Thanks, Captain Obvious. I had no idea. Are you ready? My man and me found a big 'ole secret and it has 'Collin's gonna shit his pants' written all over it."

She made it sound so appealing.

Also, I didn't want to go anywhere that had that kind of lewd graffiti on it. What kind of place had they found that was more scandalous than the one we were standing in?

"Let's go. Though I doubt there will be defecation from me or words of that manner written anywhere."

She laughed, but it was short-lived. "We'll see. This is some stone-aged shiznit. I don't even think your books covered this brilliance. Grab my hands, but don't try to cop a feel. Ari told me how you are. Second base already? Collin!"

I'd never tried to touch any female inappropriately, but Colby was just trying to get a rise out of me. I had learned, reluctantly, how to play her game.

"It was just the one time. She gave me my first brownie—made me frisky."

She stopped holding my hands and bent over in laughter. It wasn't that funny, but when I tried to fit in with their snark, I found it was always funny to them.

"You are getting better at that—not good, but better. Let's go. I told Theo to be ready with the camera."

She took my hands in hers and winked at me, which scared me more than reassured me.

In a flash, or a poof, we were in a tent—with rugs—and I swore there was a hookah in the corner, but I dared not ask questions. I was so tall that my head brushed the top of the fabric ceiling. Bending, I walked nearer to the center where the pitch was higher.

"Theo, take like a hundred pictures. I want the exact moment he finds out where we are."

I didn't want to wait or give them the opportunity to take any pictures. "Where are we? And who are these people?"

A man with an unnecessary beard stepped forward and bowed a little. "Guardian, we welcome you to our home. I'm sure you are as familiar with us as we are with you."

I chewed on the inside of my cheeks while I thought about it. "Protectors—Clandestine." At least that was the only thing that made sense.

The man clapped, and Theo continued taking pictures.

"Knock it off, Theo," I grumbled.

The man soured at my statement. "You speak to the Eidolon as such?"

Colby cracked up, snorting. "The Viking is our friend. It's okay. We're not really formal, but thank you."

A woman with raven hair stood. "I did not see a Viking, but I did see him. Is he a Viking? Can he be trusted? My visions are never wrong."

As usual, Colby found this funnier than it actually was. I did a double take looking at her now. In the glow of the lanterns, she looked worse for the wear—paler—more fragile—like she could collapse at any moment. I would have to speak with Theo about it. Maybe it was too much flashing.

"I am not a Viking. That is a special 'pet' name."

Colby snorted again. "Special is right."

The woman did an almost bow. "I am Malynn. Welcome to the Clandestine. You now help protect the Eidolon and his mate. You are no longer a Guardian."

I hadn't been a Guardian in a long time—longer than I could remember. It had only been months since Theo knocked at my door but, for the first time, contrary to what I'd always been taught, I felt like this was what I was born to do.

"Thank you. I think. Where is Ari?"

Colby turned to Theo with her palm out, extended. "Pay up. It hasn't even been five minutes."

Theo groaned and whispered something in her ear that made her defenses drop. I didn't even want to know. Contrary to her statement, no money was exchanged.

"I'm going to get her, Collin. Don't worry. Your mate will be here soon."

Theo flashed out with hardly a lick of wake. I wouldn't even acknowledge him calling Ari my mate. Colby would drag it through the mud and back again. I had learned when to give her fuel and when to stay silent.

"Colby, may I speak to you?" I asked, taking her by the arm and leading her away from the crowd.

"What?" She smiled but even it wilted.

"Is something else going on with you? Is there something I should know before the others get back?"

She looked around, flashing a smile to the others before turning her back on them. "I'm a little weaker than usual. I have no appetite. And no matter how much I try to sleep, I can't for more than a few minutes at a time. But I think it's just all that's been going on. Don't tell Theo. He's so preoccupied with going back to the Fray that he barely notices anything."

I countered her. "He needs to know. He won't return if something is wrong with you. You know he won't. His job as your mate is to take care of you."

Colby grew angrier as I spoke, gritting her teeth. "I know what his job is, and taking care of me is the smallest part. Now you shut it or I will shut it for you. Got it, Viking?"

Malynn stepped forward, and Colby raised her palm to tell her it was all right.

"I won't say a word. You have my promise. Just wait until Ari gets here. I won't have to."

Ari and Theo arrived minutes later, looking like they'd had a similar conversation—or at least as pointed.

I knew a lot of things about our friendship

situation, but what I didn't know was how to act with Ari in front of Theo and Colby. It hadn't been long since they discovered we were getting to know each other, but it was still new.

"Hey," Ari said as she walked over, encircling my waist with her arms. Colby giggled. I took it as her sort of approval, so I hugged her back and stroked the length of her hair.

"It's been a while," I said to her, bending to allow my lips to grace her ears. I didn't know what I had been so worried about. As soon as Ari looked up into my eyes, there was no one else in the room or the world.

"It's been too long. We really need to do something about that." It wasn't the time or the place, but seeing Ari again made me never want to let go. I didn't ever want to be cold again as I was when she wasn't with me.

She smiled and the cleft in her chin got deeper. "Then we'll just have to stay together."

I blew out a deep breath. "Can't get more together than being sealed." I barely got the words out. There was nothing I wanted more than to be with this woman for the rest of my life, but blurting it out in a room full of people wasn't the way I'd planned it.

Ari gasped and pulled back to look at me. There was some age difference between us, but it didn't matter. She was my mate, and I knew the Almighty had created us for each other.

"Are you asking?" She was taunting me, and I loved it.

"I am."

Colby squealed. "Sounds like sealing vows to me. Looks like we have a ceremony to plan."

Malynn stepped forward. I thought she would probably be the one to give us the reason why we shouldn't be sealed—the adversary to our union. Instead, she said, "I see many children in your future. Many, many children."

Ari shot daggers at her with one look. "One step at a time, sister. I don't even know who in the hell you are."

CHAPTER SEVEN
Theo

OVER THE NEXT FEW HOURS, INTRODUCTIONS WERE MADE and plans were put into place. There were so many teams and schemes that I felt like we were on a real-time version of that TV show, *Survivor*.

Colby wanted to trick the Synod and bring Collin with her.

I made Collin promise to take care of her while also making him promise that he would alert me if anything went awry.

Ari made Collin swear that he wouldn't be the hero.

Collin told me he would do anything to protect Colby.

Colby made me say that I wouldn't go anywhere without her.

The voices got louder by the second.

Ari was yelling at Malynn to shut up about how many kids she'd be popping out.

Omar, through the whole thing, was shining a sword that was bigger than my arms and legs put together.

Damn it all to hell, when is this madness going to end? Someone give me the immunity statue.

Colby would go to the Synod the next morning. So as with everything in our lives lately, I had to squash everything I needed her to know into one night and treat it like the last I had with her.

Every night I had with her could possibly be my last.

And I had to make it count.

She came to our room, given to us by Omar and Malynn, already yawning. After letting the fabric that made our door fall into place, she slipped off her dress and grabbed a tank top that had seen better days.

When she turned, I got a good glimpse of her body and didn't like what I saw.

Thin didn't even begin to describe the waif quality of her body. Colby was thin before— she'd purposefully stayed thin most of her life because she thought weight inhibited her flashing.

Then she started to eat with the knowledge that it had nothing to do with her ability to travel.

What I saw in my mate was something more like sickness.

It was such a dramatic change in such a short length of time that the sight of her constricted my chest. If I could, I would pull fat and muscle from my own skeleton and give it to her.

Her ribs stuck out. I could count every single one. The dimples above her butt were sunken and made her hipbones protrude. Even her fingers were nothing but knuckles—they resembled magic wands instead of digits.

She'd become skin and bones, but I'd been too busy running to even notice.

"Colby?" I breathed into the air, but it hung like a stale request.

"I know. I won't let them trick me into anything. I'm not stupid, Theo. I know they are still the enemy even if I can convince them to help us somehow."

My breaths were being stolen by how she'd changed.

"Colby." My voice was strained a little more. I couldn't give a rat's ass about the Synod or anyone else in the world or beyond.

"Did I miss something?" she said, still coming back at me with a snide attitude. "I won't get too out of hand, although they deserve anything I have to say to them. I guess I do owe them some sort of apology for believing they killed Rebekkah, but I'm not sure if I want to just yet."

I stood and walked over to her, running my fingers down the length of her arms and then down her spine before she could pull the tank top over her head. What had once been curves, softer than anything I'd felt in my life, were now rigid bumps and harsh reminders.

"Querida mia, you've missed a lot. You haven't eaten right in a while, I think. We should just stay here for a time. Forget about the Synod. Forget about the fight. Forget about running. Let's just get you back, okay? I'm sorry. We were running, and I didn't notice. Maybe I did and just didn't pay attention…"

Sighing, she leaned back against my chest. She was probably banking on the fact that we were too busy to notice the little things like her getting so damned skinny. If she turned sideways, I would miss her.

"I've tried to eat. It comes back up. I've tried everything I know how. Even water comes back up. I've hidden it from you. We have enough going on. It will be fine. It's just the stress or the constant flashing. It used to energize me, but now it wears me down. Like every time we flash, a little layer gets filed away."

When I reached around her, tears welled in my eyes. I could feel the difference in her waist, her hips, her everything. What I saw in my mate had to be more than just a few weeks of missing some meals.

"We have to fix this. You have to talk to Malynn. Maybe there's something they can do. Maybe Collin knows something."

Even her breathing was more shallow than normal. But if she wasn't eating, everything was probably working overtime just to keep her normal functions going.

She bumped her forehead against mine and placed a feather-light kiss on my nose.

"We can try after I get back tomorrow. I can't concentrate on anything until I see what we can get out of the Synod. I hate to say this, but they might be our only chance of stopping Sanctum. I just feel like there's something we are missing. Rebekkah always said that the truth isn't really the truth and we had to look beyond the façade. I just have this feeling. Honestly, I don't give a damn about myself until I at least try to talk to them. After tomorrow, I swear I'll ask them. I swear it."

CHAPTER EIGHT
Colby

MALYNN INSISTED ON LOANING ME ONE OF HER DRESSES for our visit to the Synod. No matter what those women did to our race, it was still ingrained in us to treat the Synod like royalty.

Brainwashed was more like it.

She put me in a long-sleeved top and a matching skirt of emerald green that left a little of my belly showing. She had to pin some of the skirt because my waist was nothing. If anyone looked closely, they'd want to feed me a cheeseburger. I'd kill for any food to stay down at this point.

With this outfit, the Synod would think I'd become a belly dancer in my spare time.

"May I do your hair?" All the attention from Malynn was kind of freaking me out. I felt like one of those princesses from fairy tales who needed assistance in getting dressed because doing it herself would just take too much effort.

"Oh, why?" I thought tangled was the new rebel. I'd try to put a brush through my hair, but it seemed that with the weight loss, my strands had become brittle, dry, and frail. Just like me.

She smiled at me and straightened my top—again. "Maybe I should tell you a little more about our people while I fix your hair. Once we were the protectors of the first Eidolon—sentries were probably a better name for us—but over the centuries, we've lost out on who we are, much like your grandmother, the Prophetess." She escorted me to the nearest mirror and sat me down on the carpeted floor in front of it. The mirror was inlaid with gold filigree, and I felt more beautiful just looking into it.

Our eyes met in the mirror. "You knew my grandmother?"

She smiled at me, wrangling with my knots. "I did not, but my father did. He was alive when the Prophetesses were rendered useless—useless? Is that the correct word?"

The agreement caught in my throat. "Useless, powerless, not valid. Yes, those are all correct words."

She continued. "He was there when the proclamation was made. Rebekkah wasn't the only one. She outlived them all, but she wasn't the only one when the Synod outlawed them. I believe there were three. I'm not sure. The Clandestine were once revered for our ability to serve the Eidolon and his family. Our women were servants to the queen and her daughters, and our soldiers would accompany the Eidolon wherever he went. We lived in their house, and we were fed and treated like royalty ourselves. We were more than slaves—more than workers. We were honored friends and advisors to the Eidolon's family. All of that ended when the Synod came. There are rules against seeking us out or even admitting that we still exist. Remember that when you go today. They will not appreciate your blatant ignorance of the law."

"It's not ignorance if you just told me, and I've never been a fan of their laws. Most of them aren't even made public until they deem someone a criminal. How can we obey the laws if they aren't even made available to us? The Lucents are a good race of people, blessed by the Almighty. We don't need a table full of gaudy old women telling us what to do."

Malynn laughed and tried, in vain, not to make faces about my mess of hair. "What does gaudy mean?"

"It means too much makeup. Too much hairspray. Too many long, red fingernails. Too much of everything. But even if they weren't gaudy, we wouldn't need them."

She had already gotten my hair looking halfway normal again. As she nodded, she kept adding some oil from a bottle on the table near her. I didn't even ask. At this point, pulling a Pema hairdo would be better than what I had going on. "We do not. That's the problem with all people. They think they need to be governed. But I think with all people that they will make their own justice and their own peace if those who want power would just mind their own beeswax."

I laughed so hard that tears came from my eyes. Her English was so good at times, and then she would say things like beeswax. "Business. Mind their own business. Only children say beeswax."

She canted her head and shrugged her shoulders. "Well, that explains some things. I once flashed to America to buy some hamburgers, and a man tried to flirt with me. I told him to mind his own beeswax, and he laughed so hard I wanted to punch him."

"Wait." I turned and faced her. She squealed because I'd made her ruin whatever she'd started back there. "You can flash?"

Her face reddened as she nodded. "Yes. We all can flash, even though we are Clandestine. Our males can flash too. If would be difficult for us to protect you if we couldn't. Warrior women. That's what we were once called. Your Collin should know. Now turn around or they'll think I'm not working."

She was joking, of course, but I turned around and lamented all the things about our own people we didn't know. All the books and records and laws—yet we knew hardly anything about who we were and why we were on this Earth.

We were uniformed, yet had allowed ourselves to be led. It was an equation bound for disaster from the start.

"Colby, you shouldn't cut your own hair. This piece is way shorter than the rest."

I furrowed my eyebrow. "I haven't cut my hair."

She just shrugged and continued.

Malynn took at least an hour to fix my hair, but by the time she was done, it looked like a mass of expertly spun spider webs. She'd placed gold clips at the bottom of the braids. For the first time, I looked like someone who was actually going to see the Synod.

They wouldn't know what hit them.

With the kind of mood I was in, hopefully it would be me hitting them—in the face—with that damned squeaky chair.

She smiled at my reflection in the mirror. "It is done. Let's go show everyone how beautiful you are. Yes, we will speak about your stomach and health when you get back. I think we have something to help with that, though I have some other less favorable theories." I stared at her in awe. "In here. Can't help it." She pointed with one finger to her temple.

As I turned round and round in front of the mirror, I actually felt human again. Well, like myself again. Malynn was another friend I'd gained on the journey, even in such a short time period. "Won't you come with me? I would feel better if maybe you were there to help me decipher the truth."

"Decipher?"

I smiled. "To know if they are telling the truth."

She bowed and looked at me with tears in her eyes. "I would be honored to once again be of service to the Eidolon and his mate."

"Get ready to learn American sass, sister. It's going to be rough."

It was just as easy for me to flash into the meeting room of the Synod as it was the golden room, but I thought if I wanted them on my side, the best place to start was with a little show of respect.

Except when we landed on the once-metallic tiles, the gold room didn't have the gleam it once did. In fact, it didn't have any gleam at all. The glittery wallpaper had been torn and tattered like Wolverine himself had a piss-fit right here. The chairs and ceiling were tarnished and almost rusting—like the whole place was antiquing before our eyes.

It was more like the rusty room now.

"It has changed. This was once a palace. Now it crumbles like it has been..."

I finished Omar's lament. "Like it has been forgotten."

The familiar click of heels alerted me to Regina's arrival. Soon, she was in front of us—a relic in her own right. Apparently, the cameras were still working.

"Regina?" I gasped and whispered her name at the same time.

Her eyebrows bunched and she cocked her head like a puppy who had heard a sound for the first time. "Colby? Is that you?"

"Yes. Of course it is."

She squared her shoulders and waved for us to follow her. We walked through the hallway that was now like a crumbling tunnel of horrors. Ivy grew from the cracks in the ceiling and the marble was like gravel beneath our feet. I had to hold Collin's hand not to trip. It was almost more decrepit than the tunnels I'd gone through with Sanctum on my ill-planned journey to end them.

She brought us into the meeting room. This was the place where I'd almost peed my pants, almost lost my tongue, and found my courage—all in the same room.

"What happened here?" I spoke first, the tiniest inkling of pity ringing in my tone.

"Why should we tell you? It's because of you and Theo that we are degraded to this hell."

Never mind—the pity was long gone.

I took it all in. The room looked like a

construction zone gone wrong. There was a gaping hole in the ceiling and the walls looked like they were withering as we stood. "How is it my fault you're living like this? It looks like a hurricane passed through here and you were behind on your insurance payments."

The group of women actually cackled at that.

"Oh, dear Colby. You are closer to the truth than you think. Now, before we discuss whatever you've come here to discuss, why don't you introduce us to your friends?"

Regina was stalling, but that was okay. She could stall all she wanted. From the looks of things, we weren't the ones at the disadvantage. New anything was in short supply at the Synod.

I pointed to Omar, who had already stepped forward. "This is Omar, leader of the Clandestine. This is his daughter Malynn. And you already know Collin, the cousin of Thor."

Collin cleared his throat. "Female, you test me."

Carlita stood and wasn't as surprised as I thought she would be. I wanted her to be 'I'm so glad I wore this yellow skirt' shocked, but disappointment seemed to be my thing of late.

"I thought we were just hitting a road block. You said it was a bump in the road. But this sort of proves it's more than a pothole, don't you think?" She wasn't talking to me. I couldn't pinpoint exactly who she was talking to, but she was surveying Omar like he was Tom

Hardy without a shirt on.

She sneered. "Omar, is it? The law says that you are not allowed to approach the Eidolon. He is only allowed to seek help from you."

The Synod was more worried about their rules than they were anything else. But looking at Carlita's face, I knew why. That was all the power they had. They hid behind rules that made them powerful—that made them the last decision makers—and created a race of beggars and monitored lives.

We'd just sat back and let it happen too.

Omar bowed, although I thought it was just for show. "Of course. We obey all the laws."

One day, I would learn to be that diplomatic—in my dreams.

"Then the tide has turned indeed. We've actually been waiting for this. Colby, I'm assuming you have some terms?"

Regina's eyebrows might not be on point like they used to be, but she could still confuse the hell out of me with one sentence. But I wasn't the scared little Lucent girl who used her smart mouth to cover up her blind fear of these women anymore.

Now they were speaking to the Eidolon's mate.

"You're not running this meeting, Regina. I am. Why don't you take a seat before your heels break? Those look like last season's Vuitton's."

She scoffed but did as I said, sitting down in

a chair that had seen better days.

"I believe I've figured everything out. Well, not everything, but that doesn't matter. I have the clues I need."

Collin looked at me with his eyebrows raised.

"After all this time, I was wrong about one key element. You didn't kill Rebekkah. You probably wish you did, but you didn't. So why didn't you correct me? Why let me think you did?"

Eliza, the member of the Synod who I mostly ignored because she always sat in silence, straightened her stature and cleared her throat. "We never wished to kill the Prophetess. It was ordered of us to get rid of her before she could divulge anything to you or Theodore, but we declined. This is why we are in such disarray. We were punished for our refusal. You must believe us. We have been through enough. If we had told you before, we would've surely been killed. After all of this, we have some semblance of self-preservation."

I wished she had kept silent.

The horrible part was that I did believe them. It sounded like Sanctum to have someone else do his dirty work. He was a weasel like that. That was back when he was trying to convince me that he was not such a bad guy, not with words but by working with me to try to take out the Synod.

It didn't make them any less guilty of the

crime.

"You declined? You declined? It wasn't an invitation to the prom, Eliza. This was Sanctum playing you like a puppet, and you yanking on the string and saying no to murdering my grandmother. And while we're on the subject, who thought it was a good idea not to warn us that someone was putting a hit out on her? I would've hidden her. Theo could've taken her to the Fray—something! I would've spent my life getting her away from him!"

They all looked at each other and nothing could've infuriated me more at that point. Now was the time for full disclosure. I'd had enough of their secrets and falsified propriety.

They were nothing more than the rest of us now, and they better damned well start acting like it.

"Colby, we did tell her. We warned her as soon as Sanctum left this room after almost killing all of us for not obeying his orders. She asked that we do nothing—including telling you."

I hated the fact that I was about to cry in front of these air-wasting beings, but it couldn't be helped. The tears that still stung over the death of my most precious family member, even over my mother, barreled over my eyelids and ran down my face. I'd never really had a proper chance to mourn her.

I screamed, "And you listened to her? What

specialized kind of idiots are you?"

Collin went around Malynn, who was next to me, and put his hand on my shoulder. He was making me remember, whether that was his intention or not, that this wasn't all about me—this was about all of us and I was getting off topic.

I barely reined myself in.

"Why would she do that? She was the last Prophetess." I hated how weak my voice sounded.

Eliza spoke up again, but before she started, I wanted to choke her just for the look on her face. "She said it was necessary. She said she had lived a full life, and there was no longer any use for her with our race on the cusp of a new era. I asked her questions—begged her to tell me more and to allow us to tell you and your mother, but she refused. She made me swear. She kept saying that I wasn't asking the right questions."

A swear to a Prophetess wasn't just a promise made as by child with fingers crossed. The only other more sacred promise was one made to the Almighty.

And my grandmother saying that Eliza wasn't asking the right questions was spot on—that was what she did when she thought we didn't need to, or wouldn't want to hear, her answer.

"You're a coward—all of you are. Who cares

if she told you not to tell us? You didn't even believe she was special—that she was even relevant anymore. When in the hell did you start doing what she said? You had to choose that moment to start respecting her?"

Regina turned around in her chair, but I had no sympathy for the tears she tried so hard to hide. No. She was the enemy. She wasn't crying at all. She was probably hiding a shit-eating grin.

"Colby, it isn't that easy. Rebekkah wasn't the only Prophetess in the time when we banished them. She was one of about six, but the other five were not stable. Their times were up, and they were scaring the Lucent around them. People were panicking. We had no leader. The Eidolon was less than useless. We took a stand. The only course in getting power is to stand up and speak the loudest. It just so happens that Regina has the biggest mouth of them all."

Regina turned back around and rolled her eyes. "Look, Colby. We assumed you would be here to take us down—or out, whatever the case may be. We are not the leaders anymore. Sanctum or Eidolon, those are the two choices."

I took no care in wiping away my tears and addressed them the best I could.

"We don't want a leader. We just want to be free. There's one thing no one is counting on. Sanctum doesn't know that. He thinks we are still scared of you. That you are still trying to keep us under your thumb and succeeding at it. He is *our* enemy. And either he is your friend or your enemy, but from what he's done to you, I'm assuming he's not your favorite person anymore."

Regina looked bored. "What can we do? He has all but stripped us of our powers."

I smiled, but only with one side of my mouth, which I knew made me look like the Joker. I was sure of it.

"What do you mean 'all but stripped us'? Can you still flash?" I'd assumed they couldn't because if they could, they certainly would've gotten themselves out of this mess. At least they could've gone to their homes instead of hanging out in depression central.

"We can. It's all we have. He burned our homes. My mate is missing. Eliza's children are missing. We are paying for our crimes, Colby. Don't doubt that for a second."

No one deserved those things more, but I reserved my empathy for another time.

I pushed aside all the things I hated about these women. I hated how they had used falsified information to keep me, and the rest of us, terrified. I hated how they had used what I now knew was fraudulent videos of Sevella to torture me. I didn't care what their motivation was or how much they thought it was the right thing to do—I could work with them, but I'd always see them as the enemy.

My smile faltered, but my happiness remained. "When Xoana received her gift, it was all she had. She was a poor girl with no prospects of ever traveling or even seeing beyond the fields. She was a female with the gift—the blessing. And now we are all just going to cower because some guy thinks he can run the show? Bullshit. What kind of Lucent females are we? Tell me, Regina, what kind of female are you?

I could see my words sinking in and growing thorns of revenge and strength in them. That was what we needed—for the past transgressions and what could've been. It was time for us to take our race back.

Eliza stood and pushed away the table, letting it flip over onto the ground. "Tell us what to do and we will do it. I've had enough."

Maybe that was what her silence was all about. She was building a little rebellion inside. I might just end up liking her after all.

"Well, there's a ton of us and only one of him. I need to know where he is, and I need to know where that wench Pema is. We have to find Pema. She is the key to stopping Sanctum."

Regina got up but didn't look as fired up as the others. "Why Pema?"

I took a little pride in actually knowing information before them. "Because she's in cahoots with the devil himself."

Eliza swayed while still sitting and Regina turned a vulgar color of green. They were as put off about Pema being Sanctum's accomplice as I was.

CHAPTER NINE
Theo

OMAR'S TENT PALACE WAS BIG—BUT NOT BIG ENOUGH TO have the Synod in there with us. Not nearly big enough.

"What are they doing here? You were supposed to get them on our side, but that didn't include bringing them here."

They looked more out of place in this secret place than Collin did, which was a task in itself.

Colby smiled, but it didn't work on me. Okay, it totally worked on me. "They are on our team, but we all need to be on the same page. And right now, I have no idea what page we are on. It's like building a defense team and losing my playbook. I'm stumped. I just know that the devil and his demon spawn have to be stopped, and they are pissing me off in general. You need to be free to do your job, and Pema is stupid. Plus, I can't use them if he's killed them, so they needed protection too. Can you imagine the look on Sanctum's face when he realizes he can't pinpoint the Synod either?"

Omar stepped forward. He was still treating

me like royalty, so it took him three times as long to say anything to me.

He looked at the Synod, but he didn't grin until his face was hidden from their view. "There must be some rules."

Colby flopped onto the ground next to me and leaned on my shoulder. "Rules suck. Out with them. I am the worst at following rules but for you, I'll try."

"Oh, um, most of these are for Theo. You must not take Sanctum back to the Fray. That was your first mistake. He could've taken that opportunity to grab onto you and flash into Paraiso. From there, he could attempt to take over the Almighty's army. That's the easy part."

Colby rushed him with her hand in the air, and he got the point.

"Stopping Sanctum won't be easy. You both grow weaker by the second, which is why you can't feel him anymore. You are hidden from him by the protection of the Clandestine—our magic hides this place from all. But your refusal to do your duty is weakening you, and we have yet to find out what's eating your mate."

Colby was losing steam as he spoke, but he managed a little smartass comment. "Maybe it's the same thing that was eating Gilbert Grape."

I ignored her sarcasm, no matter how on point it was. I thought Omar was going to make rules about the Synod being here.

"I can't go back to the Fray until we find out what's happening with Colby. I won't go until then." I conjured as much resolve in my voice as I could.

Omar dismissed it. "She will be well taken care of. The less frequently you go, the more souls accumulate there."

Just the mention of the Fray jabbed the knife of guilt deeper into my chest. It was all I could think about lately with any kind of clarity. "It's my job to take care of her."

He cleared his throat and did some kind of bow thing. "It's your job to take care of your responsibility. But you are no use to her or us in your state. You may be able to quell the voices for a while, but even in the short time you've been here, I can see the weight bearing down on you."

I looked down on Colby, who had fallen asleep leaning against me. There wasn't an eye in the place that wasn't on her. She seemed to be shrinking before us.

"Ari," I called, and she came to sit down next to me. "If something happens to her, I will come after you first. And then I will have to throw down with your mate because I maimed you, and then all hell will break loose. So the best thing to do is not to let anything happen to her. Are we clear?" She didn't answer immediately, so I pressed. "Ari, please. *Eu estou com medo*."

"Dude, you can't pull that shit with me. It

doesn't count if I don't know what you're saying." She looked at Collin and then said, "It doesn't matter. I would never let anything happen to Colby. You go and handle your shit and get back here. Don't make me be the one to tell her that her lover boy is never coming home. Do we have a deal?"

We fist-bumped. "We have a deal. I'll even officiate your sealing when I get back."

She beamed and her cheeks reddened. "Now we're talking. You get more flies with Kool-Aid than with pickles."

I laughed at her. Sometimes she said things like that just to get a rise out of me. "I'm leaving her while she sleeps again, aren't I?"

She nodded but switched places with me, allowing Colby to lean on her. I ignored the part of me that hated seeing her lean on anyone else. Now was not the time for ego. The time for ego was never.

Ari whispered, "Yep. Go before she wakes up. We will be here when you get back—maybe."

"Don't do anything I wouldn't do," I said and walked from the tent.

"Boring," Ari called back, and then I was gone.

I was back in the milky tide of the Fray. The weightlessness, along with the way the lack of air made my lungs seem like sponges, absorbing any drop of oxygen they could get, felt like drowning.

I listened, rolled in the silence, and then panicked.

But this time, there were no voices calling me—no hands grabbing at my clothes—no demands or pleas—no images of families lost and never found.

If Alice was a Lucent and she fell into the Fray, she wouldn't be any more confused than I was now.

And then the Almighty, with a beam of light, brighter and more illuminating than anything I'd ever seen, reached down, piercing the veil between Paraiso and the sea I was in, and appeared next to me.

"Theodore, I've been waiting for you."

CHAPTER TEN

Collin

THERE ARE SOME THINGS I WOULD NEVER TALK ABOUT TO Theo.

One was how, in the beginning, I'd believed him, but I didn't think he'd ever put his task before his personal life.

I was wrong about that.

The other was how much Colby suffered when he was gone to the Fray. She might tell him from her perspective, but watching her face when she knew he was gone was like watching a child lose their only friend.

"How long?" Colby woke not five minutes after he'd flashed away. She knew immediately what was going on. His departure may have been stealthy, but it was noticed by all.

"Just a few minutes," I whispered, scared that even the boom of my voice might shatter her.

"Maybe that's why I have a complex about sleeping. He always waits until I'm asleep before vanishing. And he wonders why I wake up so often. Asshole Eidolon. That's what I'm going to start calling him."

The collective gasp could have been heard for miles away if this place wasn't protected.

She recoiled. "I'm just kidding. I would never call him that. I'm just pissed, tired, and so hungry I think my stomach has started eating my intestines."

Malynn was brewing something—had been since we got back to the tent. She was also saying some kind of prayer or chant over the steam coming from the concoction.

She could be making magic, voodoo, or whatever as long as it made Colby better.

"It's almost done," Malynn called out as though she could hear my thoughts.

"Colby, when did this start—exactly?"

Her exhausted state did nothing to help her gather her thoughts.

"I think it was right after the wedding. The next day, he flashed into the Fray. I could still eat, but there was a weird feeling afterward. It has just progressed since then. Sometimes, I just smell food and it sickens me."

I looked straight at Ari and knew we were thinking the same thing. It seemed nearly impossible, of course, for her to become nauseated so soon afterward, but it was the simplest and most obvious conclusion.

"Colby, are we sure this isn't something physical? Like a symptom of something that could happen after you and your mate...?"

She rolled her eyes before jokingly grabbing

Ari by the collar of her T-shirt. "Translate for the Viking. He's making no damned sense, and he's crawling all over the last nerve I've got."

Ari leaned over and translated for me. Translated was a stupid word. I was just uncomfortable with the subject matter—I wasn't speaking another language.

"No way. There is no freaking way. I mean there is a way, but that doesn't happen, does it?"

Ari laughed, watching Colby. "She's gonna blow!"

I braced myself for whatever that meant.

"Not really, Collin. Calm the hell down. I'm not going to explode. You'd just love that, wouldn't you? All boys like explosions and blowing shit up."

Regina whispered to one of her cohorts, "We just thought she was sassy before."

No one else in the room knew what we were talking about, but Malynn was interested since she was the main one trying to fix it. She was staring at us and had forgotten whatever she was conjuring.

"They think I'm knocked up, Malynn."

The street slang was lost on the woman.

"Preggers, pregnant, bun in the oven, baby in the belly." Colby was smiling, at least.

"Oh... oh! No, you're not pregnant. I'm sorry." Malynn did a little bow of reverence.

"Don't be sorry. I'm so relieved. Can you

imagine bringing a baby into this? And how do you know?"

Malynn once again pointed to her temple as she did when her gift was questioned or misunderstood. "You and Theodore's children are yet to come. It is not the time."

Colby sobered. "Children? There's more than one of those things to come? Theo needs to put it away."

I looked to the heavens and begged them to make her stop.

Ari asked, "What else? What else can it be, Malynn?"

She glided through the tent, carrying a cup of something that smelled like brimstone and backside. "I'm hoping this will help. If not, I have a few more options before I try other things. I'm hoping it is something simple."

Colby sat up. "Does that taste like it smells? Because, if so, this waif thing might be okay after all."

Malynn smiled. "Trust me, the taste is heaven. Ignore the smell."

Colby grumbled to Ari. "By heaven, she means Hulk's crack."

Nothing would stop that sarcasm, but at this point, I was almost glad to hear it.

Malynn didn't hand the cup to Colby. Instead, she lifted it to her lips. Colby was not pleased to be fed like a child, but she accepted it. After the first taste, she even seemed to like it.

"It's not bad." She smiled peacefully and continued to drink, losing her posture to slouched shoulders and waning eyelids.

It was disconcerting to watch her slip into sleep like that, coaxed by whatever was in that cup.

It was what I would liken to watching someone's pain medication take effect or like a mother pulling a warm blanket up over a child—softly and so slow in its steadiness that the patient hardly noticed they were being taken under.

"Is she okay? I don't like this." Ari was holding onto Colby for dear life. Tears pooled in her eyes as she looked at her friend, both of them helpless.

"She is fine. Check her pulse. It is steady and slow. This should have her sleep for a while. When she wakes, she should be hungry."

Ari said, "Back in the states, we call that pot."

"*Ari,*" I admonished in a hush.

"What? That's what it sounds like—not that I've ever partaken."

Ari wasn't a very good liar. Or maybe she was and I didn't know it yet. I was in trouble with that one.

"Ari, sweetheart, let's put her to bed so she's not disrupted."

Ari looked at me, broken. "I don't want to leave her. I don't want her to wake up alone again."

The first lesson I learned from Ari was true friendship. She was an honorable female who, through the sarcasm and humorous jabs, would lay down her life for her friends. And it wasn't a one-way street. Colby, and even Theodore, would do anything and had done anything to keep Ari and me out of danger. They were working to make sure all Lucents were free from harm and from Sanctum.

That was friendship. It wasn't keeping score or basing love only on the good times. It was accepting a person for who they were and loving them even when who they were wasn't pretty.

People had ugly moments and ugly phases.

But if they were our friends, we loved them through it. We let them hold us at a distance when they needed to and close when they needed that as well.

Ari's ability to be the best friend was what first made me love her.

She was the most loyal person I knew.

She taught me, through actions, not through words, that loyalty wasn't just when you liked the person—it was also when you hated them, when they've pissed you off, and when they hated themselves.

Loyalty was for a lifetime.

Malynn piped in, "She will not wake up alone. I will be with her. Spend some time with your mate, Ari. Like Theo, you are no good to her when you are worn so thin. I won't leave her for a second—believe me."

Ari looked at me to gauge Malynn's response.

"She's right, Ari. We should take this opportunity to let her rest properly. Malynn won't leave her. The Clandestine are true to their word."

Ari let two of the men carry Colby's almost-lifeless body to her room. It was only when Malynn took a seat next to the bed that Ari relented her charge to Malynn's care.

"You honor the Eidolon with your care of the queen. We may need to check your lineage, Ariana. There is probably some Clandestine in your veins."

"Thanks."

We went to the room we were given to sleep in the night before. It was not as divine as the Eidolon's chambers, but I expected no less. Ours was a mix of maroons and teals. Our bed was a simple but comfortable pallet on the floor.

"You need some sleep, Ariana."

She turned, stretching out her back, and gave me a wry smile. "You heard that, huh? Ari is so much more badass."

Apparently, badass was something my mate strived for. I'd let her believe it for a while.

"But Ariana is so much more beautiful. Both are fitting for you."

She did a few yoga poses, trying to loosen

her muscles. She did that every night and first thing in the morning.

I soaked her in like a plant absorbs sunlight, growing in the knowledge of everything she did.

"Stop staring. You're creeping me out."

Ariana was a liar. From now on, in my head, I was going to call her Ariana.

"Is 'creeping me out' what the kids are calling it these days?" I loved to use our age difference as a point since everyone else seemed to tiptoe around the issue. "I mean, I am an old man, but…"

Ariana looked over her shoulder and winked. I thought my chest might burst every time she winked at me. She knew it. She knew what it did to me.

I'd allowed my age and the profession I'd grown into shape the way we had courted in the beginning.

Until Ari had kissed me.

She joked and said that if she hadn't, I never would've.

And I would not have. I was taught that those things were reserved for mated couples— not that I ever expected to be a part of one.

But she was mine.

And I belonged to her.

"Get down here, female. You've been away for far too long."

"I'm coming. Hold on." She went behind

a small screen in the corner and came out wearing one of my white T-shirts. Only a hint of a pair of shorts peeked out from underneath. She was incomparably beautiful like this—in a way that she didn't allow anyone else to see— hair down—makeup free—not giving a damn, as she liked to say.

"Creeping me out was not a compliment. But I was just kidding," she said, bending down and lying next to me on the pallet.

We lay next to each other, just enjoying breathing the same air again. Even though we had been back together for a day or so, being near her after so long apart felt like coming home. We talked about all the places we'd been since we split up, and I told her all about the California beaches. She slapped my bicep when I explained the kind of swimwear, or lack thereof, I'd seen on the beaches.

She told me she'd found the best coffee on the West Coast.

"I can't flash, but you can take me with you, right?"

She nodded. "We'll go everywhere, I promise. But what are you going to do? I can work—Lucent work, but you said you wanted to find something else to do."

I had thought about it. While I was alone, all I did was think about it. Although Ari's work would sustain a home and eventually a family, I didn't want to feel useless. I'd spent enough of my time holed up and alone.

"I think I'm going to work at a library. I would like that. There are libraries everywhere, right?"

She nodded. "Let's live somewhere with a huge library."

I'd already thought of that. "The New York Public Library is enormous. At least from what I see on the computer."

There were always giggles from her when I said the computer instead of the Internet. She'd quit trying to correct me after a while.

"I love New York. It's the answer to so many questions."

I looked down on her. She had one lithe arm behind her head and the other hand was combing through my hair. Her eyes were closed.

"What place have I never been to?"

"New York City."

"Where would you like to move when all of this is over?"

"New York City."

I sighed before asking the last one. I knew that she would stutter over the answer, just as I was over the question.

"Where's the perfect place to raise children?"

Her eyes fluttered open and connected with mine. We hadn't talked about it, but the world had been cracked open for me and it was all at my hands, anything I wanted—but what I wanted most was now in my grasp—Ariana and a family.

She grabbed the collar of my shirt, pulling me in for a quick kiss and biting my bottom lip. "Duh. New York City."

Yeah, I loved this female with everything that was in me.

CHAPTER ELEVEN
Colby

I WAS AWAKE, BUT MY EYES WERE STILL CLOSED. I KNEW where I was, but my fingers wouldn't move. I was breathing and heard someone else, not Theo, breathing next to me.

"Who is there? And I swear, if it's Collin or Regina, everyone is fired."

It sounded plain as day in my head, but out loud, it was like I was winning a really good game of Chubby Bunny.

A laugh rang out next to me, and I heard something shut like a book or a drawer. "I don't know what you said, but it sounded hostile. The only person here is Malynn—me."

Malynn was cool.

"Can you open your eyes?"

I concentrated, but she must've sewed the damned things shut.

And my mouth wasn't working, so I shook my head against the pillow. I wasn't even sure I had actually shaken it.

"Well, if you want to eat, you have to open those eyes. My dad cooked some pretty good stuff for you."

My stomach answered for her.

"Open those eyes. Let me see the blue. Our eyes are mostly brown, so we love your eyes. Oh, maybe that's creepy. Sorry."

I focused on my eyelids. Finally, after a good three or so minutes, I made them open.

"Aha!" Malynn clapped. "She wakes! How do you feel? Don't sit up yet. There may be head blush."

The things she came up with were hilarious. Always only one or two letters from the correct word. I worked my lips together until they began to work.

"Rush. Head rush. Ugh. Damn it. I could use a Slush Puppie."

"We have no puppies here."

When all this shit got straightened out, I was going to take Malynn on a U.S. tour to all the places she thought she knew but clearly didn't.

Ari walked in with the Viking and laughed. "Give me five minutes, B." In less time than that, she was back with a cherry Slush Puppie in her hand.

"He gave you a list?"

She shrugged. "When we were in Portugal. He sent me this long-ass e-mail with everything you love and all the places to get Slush Puppies. It was insane. That boy knows more about you than I know about myself."

"Forward me that e-mail," I said, taking one

long drag of the pure sugar and Red No. 40 goodness.

Red No. 40 was banned in most countries except America.

Americans loved chemicals that mimicked crack in their bodies.

"Mmmm… sugar." I felt the little hyper nerves coming to life in my brain.

"We have food for you. You've slept for three days."

I bolted up and gave myself not only a head rush, but also a brain freeze at the same time. I was just awesome. "I'm sorry, what? Three days? He's not back, Ari?"

Ari looked down and shook her head. Collin didn't look pleased about it either, although they comforted me with their opinion that he should be back any day now.

"I need…" I said, throwing the covers off the bed with the Slush Puppie going down with it. I tore out of the room. Every head in the main room turned toward me when I ran through and pushed the tent door open. I barely got outside before bending over and hurling… nothing but the little bit of red, frozen drink.

After that, there was nothing in my stomach to come out, but it didn't make me feel any less like my intestines were trying to expel the fifth horseman of the apocalypse and more.

I could hear them behind me.

She hasn't eaten in days. This is something

more than stress. Are we sure she's not pregnant?

Theo is going to kill me.

She can't afford to get much thinner.

And Ari whimpering.

It must've lasted an hour. I heaved and coughed until my body would no longer hold me up anymore. Both my abdomen and my throat felt like I'd eaten hot coals.

"It made her rest, but her stomach is still off. I have more things to try before we begin looking at other options."

"Other options," Ari repeated. But as Malynn began to unfold the answer—my knees buckled and my face hit the hot sand.

For another week, Malynn tried concoctions of all textures and flavors. At one point, I thought she was giving me sips of camel's piss from a teaspoon just to be able to say she was actually trying something different to heal me.

Whatever the last thing was, it didn't work either. There was a momentary lapse when the ebbing waves of pain ceased and I took advantage of it, asking for some bread.

As soon as I swallowed the bite of unleavened heaven, it bit back.

The pain from that little bite lasted until I could no longer tolerate it and blacked out again.

I blacked out a lot lately.

"Come on, Colby. Listen to my voice." Ari sounded like she was faking a ghost sound.

"There's no need to sing. I hear you." I groaned and then doubled over at the pain that sliced through me. "Shit, that hurts. What in the hell did Malynn give me?"

I heard several voices talking back and forth.

"Colby, I'm going to give you some more to drink. While you're under, I'm going to dig into your mind. Is that okay? You have to give me permission."

I rolled to my right side but nodded. Even if she poisoned me at this point, it was better than feeling like I was being constantly stabbed.

"I know it's hard, but you have to give me permission out loud. Speak the words."

"Dig a grave in my head. I don't care." I think I said the 'F' word somewhere in there or maybe afterward, but noticed it didn't really sound like me at all.

Malynn began chanting something like a song—a lament. It almost sounded like a melodic prayer from one of those monks.

Just when I'd almost gone to that black place again, where there was no pain, only sleep and arrested time—I felt him.

Theo was coming back. Tingles scattered over my skin. Every hair on my skin rose with a prickle.

He was near.

"Theo," I called. It wasn't a question because

there was no question that he was here.

"I'm here." One hand on my stomach and one on my forehead blotted out the pain, but not altogether. It was like a shot glass of water after four days of thirst.

But a little help was better than nothing.

"You have been gone forever." I spoke the words but didn't recognize the thought as my own. It was as if someone else was speaking through my mouth.

"It's not been forever, Querida. Only a week or so. Has she gotten any better? She looks worse." He was asking someone else in the room. Unjustified rage built in me. He was here for me. He was mine.

Why was he talking to someone else?

Why did I still feel like I was in the dark and alone, even though I could feel his hands on me, giving me a candle in the darkness?

"They've been trying to kill me." The voice took the breath from my lungs and spoke again. It was as though my lungs were haunted with a vile ghost. I opened and closed my mouth, trying like hell to make my own sentiments come out. To tell him that it wasn't me speaking. To tell him anything but the foul words that were being spoken.

"Who has been trying to kill you? Malynn? Collin? Ari?" he asked me in earnest, the precious, trusting man. It probably hadn't struck him that what I was saying didn't belong to me at all. He trusted me about anything, and now my own mouth was betraying him. Malynn spoke, and a rupture of anger and jealousy ripped through me. *How dare she speak to my mate? How dare she?*

Wait. I don't feel that way. Malynn is here to help us.

"We have done nothing but try to help her, Eidolon. I swear it. I would never do anything to harm her. None of us would. I've tried to read this situation, but it's cloudy—like this part of her life has been erased."

They hate you. It's like I always said. But you didn't listen to me, did you, Querida? Isn't that what he loves to call you? You've never been the Eidolon's mate—not truly. He was confused. He was lust-stricken. This is all your punishment for taking something that never belonged to you. It hurts, doesn't it? Doesn't it?

A pain gripped my stomach like an iron fist squeezing the juice from an orange, but the orange was my stomach.

Damn it all to hell. Either that bastard Sanctum was in my head or I was slowly turning into Sméagol—a bi-product of watching too much *Lord of the Rings* to impress Theo.

It was Sanctum, I slowly realized, and heard a foul cackle that confirmed my fear. He was inside me—speaking for me—speaking as me. If Sanctum had told Theo right that minute to kill them all for hurting me, there was a chance he would believe my voice.

Shit. I'm in deep.

It wasn't enough to have all this pain, I also apparently had to have the greatest pain in the ass of the entire world in my head...

Sanctum, is that you? Why in the shit are you in my head?

Oh, darling girl. What a foul mouth for such a beauty. Who do you think is giving you that stomach pain? The fever? The pain and anguish you haven't even told them about? You didn't want them to worry, but now it's too late. They will only hear my words through your mouth.

And believe me, it won't be anything they ever saw coming.

CHAPTER TWELVE
Theo

I THOUGHT MALYNN ONLY MEANT TO TREAT COLBY WITH herbs and general juju, but after Colby's third or fourth rant about how they were trying to kill her and how Collin and Ari were devils... and how much she hated me for what I was doing to her... I relented to the syringe Malynn held in the air meant for my mate.

"What is it?" I said, on the verge of madness myself, watching the degradation of my mate into some kind of pain-riddled insanity.

"Something to calm her. I have tried all the regular things, so now it's time to get serious. If we don't get some calories into her soon, she's going to wither away."

"You're telling me you weren't serious this whole time? What were you doing—just using her as a lab rat.

She paled. "No, Eidolon... I would never..."

I shook my head, hoping to clear it. Everything coming out of my mouth was beginning to sound more like Colby's outbursts than logical. My eyes, I knew, were glassed over in making the choice before me. I didn't want her to be knocked out, but at the same time, it was what was good for her.

Anything that got her out of pain was good for her.

Malynn put her hand on my arm. "Eidolon, I don't mean to be harsh, but if we don't get an IV into her with some nutrition, she's going to die. I've seen her future, but that can change."

"Malynn!" Omar admonished her for being so blunt, but it was what I needed right now.

She didn't falter, squaring off her shoulders and speaking with conviction. "We owe him the truth above everything else, Father. I do this for him."

I looked down at Colby's body, now a ghost of who she had been. I had to save her. My life would be nothing without her.

I nodded, saying, "Do it. Give her the shot. Give her the IV and the other thing. Do it all."

"The other thing?" she questioned. Without hesitation, she jabbed the needle into Colby's vein.

I growled at having to repeat myself, but it had nothing to do with Malynn. It was the frustration that grew inside me like a plague. "Find out what the hell is going on. Do something, for the love of the Almighty."

Already, back-up plans were forming in my mind. Selfishness took over. I could take her to Paraiso myself. There would be no more need for suffering. The Almighty would accept her.

I hadn't even gotten to tell her what he'd told me.

The life, violent as it had become, faded from her eyes as whatever Malynn had given her took over. I reluctantly moved out of the way so she could set up an IV and get fluids into her while we could.

Colby didn't move as the tube was shoved into her arm.

Everything was desperate again. We couldn't get around this life of fighting and running and constant desperation for something to just give—for something or someone to just give us a break. That was all we needed.

If there were a damned wall in this place, I would've put my fist through it. But was there? No. There were only rugs and walls made of fabric.

"I'm going to let her get a little stronger before I try to reach into her mind. Those women have been waiting for you in the main room. I'm assuming they know something or are up to something. I would be able to tell you which, but I don't want to leave her yet."

I agreed with a nod and looked at Colby one more time before leaving. There was nothing I could do by watching her suffer—but I could go after the bastard that made us run in the first place.

When I entered the main room, I'd thought

the women of the Synod would be cowering in the corner. They were once my enemy.

Or maybe they never were.

I wasn't sure anymore.

"Eidolon, I know you have just recently returned, but we would like to have a word with you."

They called me by the title. I'd gotten used to it, finally, from everyone else, but hearing it from Regina was like hearing a hated teacher speak praise.

It was just—weird.

I waved her off. "It's fine. Have you discovered anything?"

They looked at each other. The one named Eliza cleared her throat.

"Sir..."

I interrupted. "Theo is fine. Formal titles aren't necessary. Calm down, Collin." I didn't have to look behind me to know that he was going to interject some history lesson about how 'The Eidolon shouldn't be called by a nickname'.

"I didn't say anything," he answered from behind me.

"You didn't have to. Now, Eliza, continue."

It took a few seconds for the shock to wear off. "We believe we have found either Sanctum's hideout—or somewhere he once used as a place to hide. It seems he hasn't been there in a while, but there are signs of a woman. We thought maybe the woman, Malynn, could get some vibes off it or whatever she does."

"What would be the signs of a woman?"

Eliza cleared her throat. "There are women's clothes there—dresses."

Even I wasn't all that clear on what Malynn did, but I wasn't sure even she could sniff a dress and find someone.

"Where is it? Maybe I can go first and..."

"Don't even think about it, Theo." Collin again—the rat bastard—always in my junk. I smiled in spite of my thinking. He was loyal to a fault. I was sure that, given the opportunity, he would put himself in front of a bullet for me.

Hopefully, there wouldn't be bullets.

Sanctum probably didn't even know how to use a damned gun.

"As soon as Colby is stable, we will investigate that. Are there any other leads? Have you checked other places?"

Regina showed me a list she had in her pocket, with some items checked off. They were being careful to go to the places at night, so waiting for time zones was an issue that left them here and stagnant for a while.

"We are working on it. We will find him, Eidolon."

I hefted out a weighted breath—one laced with the weight of a thousand worlds—and nodded, acknowledging they were trying. Maybe they weren't so bad after all.

Or—they could be setting me up to be trapped by Sanctum.

I told them I would go, but Omar would be going first to make sure The Synod weren't, well, being the Synod again.

That was what they were infamous for, after all.

"Collin, Ari, can I see you for a few minutes?" Omar got up, ready to follow. "Alone, please?"

Omar looked hurt. While I trusted him, I needed my friends at that moment.

They followed as I walked outside, letting the hot night breeze warm my cheeks and body. It felt so cold with Colby not well.

Everything was off with her not standing beside me.

I made sure we walked out far enough not to be overheard.

There wasn't anything in particular I wanted to tell them. I didn't actually know what I wanted. Yes, yes, I did.

I wanted to lean on my friends when I was feeling like shit.

Because seeing Colby like that felt like drowning in water that I'd filled the tub up with myself.

"What is it?" Collin asked, standing in front of me. He was probably blocking the expression on my face and my lips from being read by those inside the tent.

They didn't need to see my weakness.

They needed a leader—at least for a while.

"It's nothing. I—Colby."

"Shit," Ari whispered. She grabbed Collin's arm to move him closer while she wrapped her arms around my shoulders. The first tears since I'd been back fell. I didn't know what to do. She was in there, almost lifeless, hanging on by a thread of morphine-induced normalcy. It was everything I'd never wanted for her.

And with all the powers I had, there was nothing I could do to help the one I loved the most. Flashing didn't help her. Sticking my face through windows and walls didn't help her. And what the hell good were those powers or gifts if they didn't help me now when I needed them the most?

"What do I do, Ari? I can't lose her. I can't. I won't."

She fisted my shirt at the shoulders. "We are not going to lose her. We—are—not. But I'm telling you, something hellacious is going down with her. She doesn't feel those things she's saying. I know she doesn't. It's impossible. Maybe it's just the pain. Pain makes people say things that they otherwise wouldn't. This could be something simple. I mean, we are in a tent—it's not like we have state-of-the-art technology and hospitals. This could be something completely unrelated."

I knew all of those things, but it was good to hear someone else feel the same. This was why we were given Collin and Ari in our lives.

I wiped the tears from my face with a good deal of violence. "Shit. I didn't mean to cry. Damn it."

Ari winked at me. "It's okay. I haven't really seen you cry in a while. Not that you ever cried all that much. But if there was a reason to, your mate is a damned good one."

I let the salty, hot wind of the desert dry my face. I wished Colby could see the moon. The desert made everything clearer. Except how I could save my mate? Seeing the way the world rounded made me feel small—smaller than I already felt.

"Let's go back. I've been gone from her too long."

I went in. The two new lovers stayed outside, probably to make out. That was what I would've been doing with Colby if I was a regular person and if she was not on the verge of death.

I got back to Colby. Malynn was next to her, on her knees, rocking back and forth, chanting and singing something that seemed to infuse the air with magic and soul. The air was different in that room, thick like syrup with emotion and heartache. The octaves coming from Malynn were almost holy—angelic in their rises and falls.

Her father whispered next to me. "She's calling out to the Almighty. Like you, her strength and her power comes from above. She asks him to attend her—to guide her so that she may help your beloved as He would wish it."

I nodded at Omar's assessment and stayed still and silent, careful not to disrupt her.

Her black hair and coffee skin glimmered in the light of the candles she'd lit. They were all shapes and colors, flickering back and forth as though the desert wind blew them from the outside.

I had a feeling they weren't just for decoration.

Her prayers and songs grew more and more quiet and as they did, the rise and fall of Colby's chest did as well. Her chanting seemed to lull Colby into relaxation.

For a while there, Colby was breathing like one of those zombies from *I Am Legend,* and nothing was scarier than that.

"She's breathing okay now," Malynn said, still hugging her own torso.

Omar stepped forward so that he was standing shoulder to shoulder with me. "Her prayers are not regular prayers. They are songs, like those of David, from her heart to the Almighty's ears. It's not like us, where we think about other things or let our minds wander to the day's events. She's almost in a trance, a piece of time that no one else can touch. She started this when she was about three. We thought she was a little..." He made the swirling finger around the temple gesture for crazy. "Then she told us things that no one else could know. She told us that we should listen to my mother's stories that day. So we all sat around and listened as she told us stories of how the Clandestine came to be. My mother died the next morning. That's when we knew that she was something beyond unique."

Then, like a light switch had been flipped, Malynn stopped.

"She is okay now. The pain is lessened and her breathing is better. I've put her into a coma of sorts. She gave me permission before, but I have to ask... Can I go into her mind—see what's happening?"

It seemed incredulous for her to ask me. Yes, Colby was my mate, but her body and her mind was her own. "If she gave her permission, then that's all you need."

Malynn got to her feet. "I need to eat and get a little rest. I'll come back in a few hours and begin. And... Theo?"

I wasn't the only one to notice it was the first time she'd said my first name.

"Yes?"

"It won't be pretty. It's going to be ugly. I may say things out loud that you don't not want to hear—things she probably never wanted anyone to know. But we all have those demons, you know? We all have things that no one needs to know. We all have things that no one else wants to know about us—the little bit of devil inside. I will try my best to be quiet, but if I do, don't think any less of her. Don't hate me or her when this is over."

I touched Malynn's shoulder before she could leave the room. "I would never hate you or my mate. None of us are perfect, especially me."

She smiled and looked back at Colby before going to take her rest.

CHAPTER THIRTEEN
Sanctum

THE PLACE WAS A WRECK. THOSE WOMEN HAD NO RESPECT for their own place of business.

Oh, no, wait, that was me. I had no respect for the Synod or their snotty headquarters. That was why I'd called on the demon Theo stupidly gave back to me to shake things up a bit—like earthquake shake things up.

They hadn't been here in days, that I knew for sure. Their closets were bare, and there was rotting food in the kitchen. Walking around here was like taking a tour of a tomb.

I knew where they were.

They were with him, my golden child of a brother.

And they were probably trying to find me.

At least they didn't know about Pema yet, and they wouldn't.

Grinding my teeth against the gnawing in my chest, I slammed my fist into the wall at the thought of them finding her. Plus, the fact that they had sided with him after everything we'd done for him—me and the devil himself.

It was all falling to pieces.

All of it—my plan—my ultimate goal of ending the humans—there was nothing left of it. And it was his fault.

The one person I'd turned into a monster to defeat was, inch by inch, cutting off all of my plans.

I had turned into him—the first Sanctum—the first Eidolon—all of them together. I was hiding in filthy places, trying to keep Pema and the fetus safe. I slinked in shadows and out of public places as though I was scared of him.

Pema wasn't handling it well.

She was miserable, and hiding was bad for her health.

All I had left was the hold I had on Colby and the powers that were ever growing in Theo. Which meant that there were more powers growing in me.

My master was watching.

He probably wasn't pleased.

I flashed back to Pema—in the cave on the side of the mountain that straddled Russia and Mongolia. It was a pathetic place to keep her, but it couldn't be helped. I was powerless against whatever tactic they'd found to hide themselves. But we were exposed, or so I thought. They could find me in an instant.

But if they could, why weren't they?

I was the rat that had, for so long, been the cat.

And being prey wasn't my jam.

I went to the side of Pema's bed. She didn't get up when I flashed into the room. I didn't see how the female didn't wake up. My wake was brighter and redder than I'd ever seen it, despite how much flashing I'd been doing. She was pale. The times she had looked at me lately, her eyes were glassy and her gaze seemed to go right through me.

"Are you okay?" I asked. The question was foreign in my mouth. The only reason I cared was because of the fetus—the baby—whatever.

She nodded, eyes still closed.

"What's the matter with you now?"

She turned her head away from me. Her hair was getting longer. To anyone that didn't know, it would seem like she had just cut her hair this short, but comparatively, it was longer.

When she did speak, her voice could barely be heard. "I hate what you're doing to Colby. If I had known, if I had known this was how it had to be, I would've denied you. You said this was your chance for redemption, but it's just an excuse for you to torture her because she…"

"Don't say it. Don't you ever say it." I ground the words through my teeth, courtesy of a clenched jaw.

"It's true. I might not say it, but that's what this is all about—always has been. I thought giving you a child would make you love me. I've never regretted anything more in my life."

107

I left her there with alligator tears falling down her face. Her belly had swollen a little, but there was still seven more months until the baby was born.

I didn't know whether I could take seven more months of this earthly hell.

CHAPTER FOURTEEN
Ari

"THERE. DID YOU SEE IT?"

Collin was losing it too. I didn't see a damned thing. All there was in this place was sand, sky, sun, and moon—there was nothing else. I'd gladly welcome the facade of a mirage at that moment—if mirages had Dr. Pepper and spicy Funyuns.

"No. I'm sorry, Collin. What am I supposed to be seeing again?" I leaned against his side while his arm was draped over my shoulder. No matter who was chasing us or what lay ahead, I knew that Collin would keep me safe.

He continued to stare into the sky. "It was like angry lightning. Red, bright as hell. It's him. It was far away. To a human, it might look like airplane lights or one of their infamous UFOs. But it was him. I'd recognize that lightning anywhere."

"Sanctum? Why is his lightning red? Wait, can't anyone's lightning be red if they are angry enough? It could be anyone."

Collin chuckled. It made my whole body

shake. "His lightning is red all the time because he's the devil. What do you expect?"

The Sasquatch had a sense of humor. I had to admit, sometimes, he was funnier than I was. This was not one of those times.

"I feel selfish," I admitted, leaning even more toward him, taking in his scent and reveling in it.

"Why?"

I breathed into the night. "Because all of this is going on and the only thing I can think about is that we won't be able to be sealed until Colby is better—until Sanctum is, well, whatever is going to happen to him—and Theo is not in the Fray. If he is going to seal us, we have to pick a time when he isn't being called by the voices. If we were human, we would go elope in Vegas and have it done with. Sometimes, I wish our life was easier—normal even."

He turned, placing his hands on either side of my face. "That's not how you want to do it. You and I both know that. You want a dress and a ceremony just like everyone else. If we are going to do this, then we need to do it right. And we are going to do it because I can't live without you in my life any longer. And you can't live without me. You'd get cold."

He joked, but it was all true.

There was no way I could live without Collin for another day.

CHAPTER FIFTEEN
Colby

It's too damned crowded in this place.
And by this place, I mean my brain.
And by my brain, I mean that thing in my head
that used to belong to me.
Apparently, it has two extra tenants now and
the bastards aren't paying rent.

I HAD TO FOCUS. MALYNN HAD JOINED OUR LITTLE SEESAW ride and was now playing hide and seek with Sanctum. It was like having annoying little fire ants under my skin—next to my skull—right next to the cortex.

Malynn. Malynn, can you hear me? Do you hear him? Do you see him?

For that outburst, I was given a shock of pain from the other occupant. He sucked at the roommate thing.

Shhh… I've got this.

Such slang for a girl who frequently missed words.

It was like one of those surgeries, where

they numbed it, but they said a little pressure would be felt. Except this was a whole hell of a lot more than pressure. There was pain and anguish. He overrode most of what I wanted to say.

And Malynn was there too. She wasn't as unwelcome, but she was still just as weird. Her presence was a ghost, gliding in and out of my consciousness like a desert wind through my memories.

I knew she could see everything, and the guilt that came with it almost consumed me. There were the memories of Theo and me, and the way I'd broken his heart time after time—all the while knowing exactly what I was doing.

The selfishness.

The conceit.

The deceit.

And everything in between.

She saw it all.

There was a twinge of knowing as she delved into my memories since I found out Theo was the Eidolon.

All the things I didn't want anyone to know.

Everything I'd thought was forgotten.

In a swift move, so fast I barely noticed the action, she was gone. There was a space no longer occupied by her, and I wondered if he'd gotten to her too.

I wondered if anyone would ever get me out of this.

CHAPTER SIXTEEN
Theo

I WASN'T SURE WHAT I WAS THINKING, BUT THE SCENE IN front of me wasn't it. Malynn had passed out right after gasping and holding her own throat like she was choking.

Omar and his son had rushed in to care for her.

Even through it all, Colby never stirred.

"Is she okay?" I asked Omar.

"She is fine. She's waking up now." He'd put something to Malynn's nose—a bottle that she had at the ready near where Colby lay. She must've known something like that was going to happen.

Of course she did. She knew everything that was going to happen. Time after time, I'd thought about asking her what happened to us—to me—to the Lucent race, but it didn't matter what she saw. We were in charge of our destiny, and we could change it at any moment.

Looking back, I realized I had agreed to the process of Malynn delving into Colby's mind without asking if she'd done it before and how much risk was involved.

Though I couldn't say I would've disagreed with her going forward with it even if there had been risk.

It was all worth it to save Colby.

Malynn stared into the air for almost a half an hour, silent and still. She said that she might mutter things out loud that were in Colby's mind, but she did none of that. I was relieved. Colby and I had been through too much. From my standpoint, anything that needed to be forgiven had been long forgiven and forgotten.

Like none of it had ever happened.

"What's happening?" I asked, not being able to stand the silence anymore.

Malynn jolted at the sound of my voice. "Eidolon," she said, and then sat straight up. "We have to help her now. He's taking over everything. He tried to trap me inside of her mind. He's there, conducting it all—the pain, the hurtful words coming out of her mouth, her starvation, and her worry—all of it. He will strip her of everything physical, mental, and emotional until there is nothing left to wake up to. Even if she did come out of this, if we allow him to continue for much longer, she will be a shell of her former self."

I knew who the *he* was. It was always him. Anything negative that happened in our life was because of him.

My knees slammed to the ground in rage.

"How? How is he doing it? How can I stop him? Get him out of there!"

"No," Omar protested, still holding his daughter's hand with the worry of a father written all over his face.

I begged, out of breath. "Tell me how to stop him. How does he have this hold on her?"

Malynn shoved the heels of her hands against her eyes and cursed. "He has something of hers. He's using it to manipulate her."

I thought about what he could have. It could be anything. He was with us in the house of Xoana. He could've taken her clothes, her belongings, or anything else he wanted.

"He could have anything."

She shook her head. "Not just anything, Eidolon. It is something from her—something of her. It's like a piece of her skin or something else. Maybe blood? I don't know. As soon as I saw his hold on her was that intense, he tried to kill me—not physically, but he was going to trap me in her mind. But I will tell you one thing, brewing below the pain and anger, there was desperation. I think hurting Colby is the last straw—it is the last way he knows to get what he wants. I don't know what it is."

The only thing I could think of when she said skin was that handmade ninja star made by the creature on *Jeepers Creepers*, the second one. It had a piece of belly button in the middle.

"How in the hell would he have gotten her

skin? And don't you think she would've noticed if Sanctum walked up and cut a piece off her? I'm pretty sure she would've nut punched him."

Malynn rocked back and forth. She was obviously disturbed about the things she saw in Colby's mind, but I wouldn't dare ask about it all. I didn't want to know, and I didn't need to.

If she knew half the things that went on in my mind, I would be single in a heartbeat.

I knotted my fingers in my hair, strung out with aggravation. There was no time. Whatever Sanctum was doing to her was killing her from the inside out.

He had to be stopped.

But I knew him. He wouldn't come of his own choice, and I didn't want him anywhere near these people or to know where we were.

"Malynn, please stay with Colby. The rest of you, we need to gather in the main room. I have something to say."

It took under a minute for everyone to gather. I stood before them. Probably for the first time, I really recognized the power my words and plan would have on them and our race. They needed me to lead them—at least for now.

And I was no leader without Colby.

Clearing my throat, I prepared to make a speech I never thought I would have to make. Standing there felt artificial to me.

"My mate's mind and body have been

infiltrated by Sanctum. He has something of hers that is allowing him to control her and bring her great pain. He is starving her to death and driving her to madness at the same time." I paused, not believing what I was about to say about the man who was once my brother—my best friend—someone I'd looked up to since I was a boy.

"Sanctum is a coward. Even if I tell him where we are, he won't come. I am left with no choice but to play by his sanctimonious rules. Everyone in this tent who can flash needs to look for Sanctum's hideout. He has a woman with him. She has short hair and is a few months along with the child of Sanctum." There was a collective gasp, and I let it all die down before continuing. "She is our only leverage against my—against him. Find her. Find her now before Colby dies. Bring her to me. Because if Colby dies—I will die with her."

I made sure to meet every single person's eyes before leaving the room. I'd made the orders, but I was no general. They would have to form their own teams and do their own work.

That was what the final goal was—to have the Lucents rule themselves.

Before I'd left the room, Collin had become what I'd always known he could be. With a booming voice, I heard him break up the crowd into teams of three. The sounds of maps being unfolded cut through the voices.

He could handle the logistics.

When they found Pema and brought her to me, my work would begin.

CHAPTER SEVENTEEN
Sanctum

IT WAS TOO QUIET. EVERYTHING WAS TOO DAMNED QUIET.

CHAPTER EIGHTEEN
Collin

MY LIBRARY ORGANIZATIONAL SKILLS WERE FINALLY coming in handy. Setting up plans to seek out Sanctum wasn't easy, but there were just so many places he could hide. I had Regina, Omar, and Omar's brother start out in the first logical place—where I'd last seen the red lightning.

In case they didn't know what he looked like, I snagged Ari's phone and showed them a picture of him before she had added the horns and pointed tail to send to Colby. She took the phone and showed them both versions, which lifted their spirits a little.

Theo had given us the news that none of us wanted to hear. Colby was as important to the people surrounding me as he was. Because we all knew that without her, he was like the Tin Man without a heart.

Sanctum would pay for what he had done to all of us. It seemed surreal that one person could cause so much damage to a race. He'd taken powers from the people and blamed it on our leaders. They had fallen victim to his schemes and threats, losing the respect of the Lucents.

Singlehandedly, Sanctum had almost put the Lucents on the path to extinction.

He had to be close. He wasn't smart enough to find a place we wouldn't look.

Everyone filed out with the explicit instructions to come back at once if they saw Sanctum or thought they saw the woman. We didn't have any pictures of her, so they would be stabbing in the dark.

They were each given three or four locations to flash to, search the area, and then report back so I could take inventory of where we were supposed to go.

But it wasn't enough. And it sure as hell wasn't fast enough.

"Eidolon," I called to Theo. Understandably, he was shaken and nearly comatose at Colby's current state. He was quiet and pensive. He stared into the abyss of the desert and never before had I ever seen him look so lost.

"Hmm?" he said, but he never moved from his stance.

"We need the others. The more people there are searching for him, the easier and faster it will be to find him."

His black hair was longer. When he turned his head, it fell into his eyes, but this time, he did not correct it. Appearance was last on our lists of priorities.

"There are no others. This is it, Collin. What others?" Irritation laced his tone.

"There are many others, Eidolon. You and your mate have restored the gift to many. I watched you with my own eyes. I saw their gratitude. If you call on them, they will answer. I cannot flash or I would go myself. You can ask this of them. The Eidolon can ask this of his people. They will not deny you. They love Colby just as much as we do."

He tipped his chin back and raised his face to the heavens. Words were spoken, but no sound left his mouth. My only knowledge of it was his lips moving.

"He gave me a choice, Collin."

I held my ground. "What choice? Who?"

He remained silent for a few more moments. Soon, his attitude was chased away by a fake smile and a new upbeat attitude. "Nothing. Forget I said anything. Do you think they will come? Yes. Yes, they must come. They will come. All I have to do is ask them. Will you come with me, Collin?"

I looked around. What I was doing was purely logistical. Even a buffoon could do it. And from what I'd seen in the faces of those Lucents who had been restored by the Eidolon, they wouldn't hesitate in helping him.

Some of them might offer to kill Sanctum themselves.

I nodded. "I will go with you, Theodore. You

know that."

He held up one finger to me, and I waited as he checked in on his mate. There was no need for me to ask how she was after seeing his face come back with the same hollow look.

His voice cracked as he spoke, "Let's go. The faster we find him…"

I finished his sentiment. "The faster he goes down. I'm willing to bet anything that Pema is the only piece we'll need to take him out."

Theo looked at me, really looked at me, then nodded and grabbed my arm. "Collin," he said. "I am betting everything on that. I am betting everything on the fact that my brother was stupid enough to make that investment—and that he will come to claim it."

We flashed straight to Nebraska, the first place Colby realized how many people she could touch through her connection to the Eidolon. Sway and her new mate now oversaw the place, making sure that Sanctum didn't come in and try to wipe them all out.

"Sway?" Theo saw her first. Sway ran as hard as she could to Theo, hugging him with all her might but immediately noticing the difference.

"Where is Colby?" she asked. Her voice broke with the question.

Theo tried to smile at her, but even his mouth was saddened. "Sanctum is inside her. Somehow, he has infiltrated her mind. He's giving her all kinds of pain and controlling her thoughts. That's why we need you. We need all of you." He projected his voice out to reach the gathered crowd.

The woman, I couldn't remember her name, who had first questioned Colby's power, stepped forward. "Where is she? Where is your mate?"

Theo explained in detail the events leading up to his arrival. As he progressed in the story, he withered in spirit. The people gasped and gritted their teeth in the appropriate places and more than one hand reached up to wipe tears away.

By the end, he was done—physically and from what I could see, mentally. We had to do this for him. We needed to be his strength when he could barely hold himself up.

The woman turned to the crowd. "We will all help—all who are able. Some need to stay to protect the children. All able Lucent women come forward. Our leader needs our help. Colby needs us. She is our sister and the one who came when we thought all was lost. We won't let you down, Eidolon, either one of you."

There must've been hundreds, maybe on the cusp of a thousand, women who did not hesitate in coming forward in mere minutes. They all pledged their undying allegiance not to Theo or to Colby—but to bringing down Sanctum.

And if Sanctum thought he was in trouble

before—he was really in hot water now. There was a gang of Lucent women on his tail.

Pissed-off Lucent women.

Women whom he had stolen their very essence from.

And it was well known what they said about hell having no fury...

CHAPTER NINETEEN
Theo

Days had passed. It seemed like every clue led to nothing—and nothingness led to the next empty clue. And every day, my hope dimmed.

"It's like that game," Ari said, scouring the map for a new place to go. "You know, where you hit that rat that pops up? Eventually, there's a pattern. He won't break from his pattern because right now, it's working. All we have to do is find it."

No one, including Collin, was working as hard or as diligently as Ari. When she wasn't glued to the map or flashing around the world, she was at Colby's side, talking to her—reminding her of who waited for her on the other side of the pain—on the other side of madness. She told Colby stories, trying to make her good memories come forward.

I bet that Sanctum was doing his best to refute every one.

"Yeah, but how in the hell do you find the pattern of the devil?"

She all but ripped the large, red marker from

Collin's hand and went to work. "He's been in Russia, Mongolia, New Zealand, Uruguay, Greenland, and The Dominican Republic. He's sticking to little countries, which is stupid. They would be safer and less obvious in the more populated countries. Even when he was in Russia, we found that little cave in the side of the mountain. That's where Collin saw the red lightning coming from. I think we are going about this all wrong. We are hunting him when all we have to do is watch, listen, and trap. His lightning is bright, red, and vibrant. He can't hide it. We need Lucents in all corners of the world. But you need to tell them to stop looking. They need to look to the sky and wait for him to light it up."

Collin chuckled. Ari shot him the dirtiest look since Clint Eastwood.

"That's it? You didn't need to take my marker for that. Your answer is to wait for him? Give me my marker back, female."

He was lucky she put the top back on the marker before she chucked it at his face.

"Yes, we wait. Bad guys always return to the scene of the crime. He's not creative. He's not using all of his options. Eliza found evidence that he returned to that shack in New Zealand, the one where Theo was hiding for a while." She gasped and did a dance, coupled with some kind of muppet flaily arms. "Wait a damned minute."

She turned and waited for Omar to finish his conversation with a tapping foot and impatient arms crossed over her chest. "Omar, I know that we are protected here, but can Theo project his weird shadow person out of here? If he did, will Sanctum be able to sense it?"

Omar looked at me. I hoped he didn't think I had the answers.

He chewed on the question a few more seconds before asking, "You know where it is when you send it out? It does what you command, correct?"

I nodded.

"Then he should have some piece of that gift. I don't think he can create his own shadow, but he might think that shadow is you. It might be enough..." His voice trailed off.

"Enough to what?"

Ari smiled like a cat that saw her mouse. "Enough to trap him into flashing there. And wherever he is, the shaven-haired wench will be."

I took in her plan and mulled it over a while. It just might work. My chest warmed with the knowledge I held about the entire situation.

What he didn't know, what none of them knew, was that if I wanted to, I could end it all—end me—end Sanctum—and wait for Colby in the beyond. But she deserved life.

She deserved everything life had to offer her.

First, he would fix Colby—and then he would die.

CHAPTER TWENTY
Colby

Mmm... He cooed in my mind. His words slithered through my conscious like a slug along the ground, leaving trails of discomfort and dirtiness. *That person you let in was onto something. I think she's got me figured out, Princesa. Shame on you—just opening up your mind like that to anyone.*

I mentally gagged on his words. They were filthy and wound through my veins like slime. More and more, he had begun to speak to me in Portuguese.

I hated it.

Even more, I hated that he might've ruined the language for me forever. If Theo said anything to me in Portuguese, even in love, from then on, I might not be able to handle it.

Do you see the flaw in my plan yet?

For days, maybe hours, I didn't know time anymore, Sanctum had told me every detail of his plan to make Theo give him access to Paraiso—including bringing me to the brink of death in the process.

What he didn't think of was that Theo's loyalty to the Almighty ran far deeper than his loyalty to me. I'd known it all along and had accepted it. More than that, I knew that his choice was the way it should be.

No, I answered, but of course, I did. The thing that Pema didn't know was that the baby she carried would never be hers or his. It would never be hers because the birth would kill her, and Sanctum knew that before he… ewww.

She would die trying to find someone to love her or searching for some kind of meaning in all of this.

It would be the death of her.

She would die giving birth to the son of the man who wanted to end us all.

What a way to go.

The flaw is… your darling Theodore isn't doing anything to save you. He's traveling back and forth to the Fray, rescuing those idiots who got stuck. Oh, and you know what else? He has a new friend—someone not as… needy as you. She's got her own powers, that Malynn. Plus, now she knows all your devilish little secrets. Poor Theodore probably needed a good shoulder to cry on after he heard all the things you've been thinking about him—about all of this—about me.

Sanctum was an idiot if he thought I was going to believe any of his bullshit. Theo was loyal to a fault.

But it had been days since I last heard his voice…

And if Theo lets you die—who will raise my little devil?

CHAPTER TWENTY-ONE
Theo

"Can she hear me?" I constantly sought answers from Malynn on Colby's state. She swore to me that she saw no reason why Colby wouldn't be able to hear me, but I had my doubts.

Or had Sanctum somehow stopped her from hearing my voice?

"She can, I believe."

The 'I believe' part was new.

We sat on either side of Colby's body, now getting nutrients and fluids through an IV around the clock. Sanctum might be able to bring her pain, but Malynn's medicine was at least keeping her knocked out.

Sighing, I just hoped it wasn't keeping her out without relieving the pain.

Malynn spoke, "I hope Ari's plan will work. She is certainly passionate about it. I've never had friends. But if I had them, I would want them to be like her and Collin. I thought we Clandestine were loyal, but your people would do anything for you—even the Synod seems to have changed their ways in seemingly a short amount of time."

Sending my shadow out in Scotland seemed so strange. It was about the only place that Colby and I hadn't gone. Neither had Sanctum. Plus, I hadn't sent the shadow out in so long that it felt strange, like peeling my skin from my body.

"I think it will. I'm pretty sure he is already locked on to the shadow's location, but whether he will fall for the trap is another thing."

Malynn sighed and pushed a hair behind Colby's ear. "I hate that the smart ones are usually the bad guys. Ever notice that? They should use those smart brains for something nice."

I chuckled at her assessment. It was true, of course.

"She needs to be bathed. She has been laying here for almost two days, sweating. Let me go get some hot water and soap and I will be right back."

"No." I stopped her with my palms out. "Let me. This is my mate."

Malynn opened her mouth to argue, but I was having none of it. I grabbed a large bowl from the bathing area and filled it with warm water from a pot that was kept over a fire, along with a towel, a sponge, and soap.

If she were with me, Colby would've probably complained about the soap smelling like sandalwood.

She hated the smell of that and patchouli.

She said patchouli reminded her of a stoner girl in high school who committed suicide.

I walked back in and set up before running everyone off. Malynn was having a conversation with Collin and Ari about me not allowing her to do her duty.

"Malynn, your job is to protect and serve us, correct?" She nodded. "And while I respect that, there is no one on this Earth who can care for my mate like I can. Not even you."

For a split second, she was offended. Then her face softened. She understood.

"Everyone out. Colby would be really pissed if I started stripping her in front of the Viking. He had the hots for her in the beginning— there was shameless flirting. Although, now that I think about it, we know there were some questionable naked moments between Ari and Colby while I was gone. I'm not even going to ask about those. Collin, you might want to find out the down low on that before mating this one."

Collin looked offended, but then blushed.

Ari held up two fingers with one hand while the other one was busy making her point, fisted on her hip. Collin was behind her, barely keeping his composure. "There were two shower incidents. And both times, I was rescuing her from her crying her eyes out because you left her again." A gasp chased her words. I didn't think she intended to reveal so much. "Theo, I'm..."

I turned away. I couldn't look at her anymore. It wasn't her fault. It was mine. "Just go, Ari. I need to take care of her like I haven't so many times."

It was a dig, and Ari didn't deserve it. That was what happened sometimes. Friends were trusted to be there through thick and thin, so words and emotions got spilled onto them without censor.

Real friends knew when you were saying bad things because of self-righteousness

The rest were just there for the good times—or to take advantage.

I knelt next to my mate, my love, and my heart, ready to happily fulfill one of our sacred vows, to care for her in times of sickness. It was an honor that I'd never wanted to fulfill. "Colby, meu amada. I'm going to undress you now. You've been wearing this dress for more than one day. I know that if you could, you'd have been out of it a long time ago." I started at the small straps at the top of the dress, moving them down her arms. Malynn had unhooked her IV, so I had to move quickly.

"Meu coração, I have to tell you some things while I have you to myself. Ari told me how much you cry when I leave for the Fray. She didn't mean to. I knew that you were sad, but I assumed you were okay. You've always been

135

okay without me. Isn't that right? I can't say that my decision to do what I had to would've changed, but *como tu me podes perdoar*. There will be a time, soon, when you won't have to worry about that anymore. You won't have to cry while I'm gone to the Fray. You will stop missing me one day. I know what I have to do now. I know how to stop all of this. *Vai depressa terminar*. I promise you that, Querida."

Sliding the dress off her skeleton form, I bit down on the inside of my cheeks to keep from gasping or making any other kind of noise that she would hear as shock. She didn't really need to know that I was completely aghast at what she had become in such a short amount of time. She wasn't any less beautiful or strong. In fact, she would emerge from this stronger. But saying that was wrong too.

Who wanted to hear that when they were going through something?

No one. That was who.

I focused on telling her what would be.

"Ah, my love, you will see. I have a plan that no one sees coming. They don't know that my way of ending Sanctum will be swift. He won't be anything but a deflated version of what he is now. He will be left breathing—but I will kill him at the same time. Let me tell you why, Querida. He deserves so much more than death. Death would be a welcome release after what I'm going to do to him."

I washed her hair first, the best I could, washing away the sweat from her spasms and cries for help. Strands of her blonde locks came out in my hands and the rest of it was thin like spider webs.

"He took from our people and I will take from him."

Moving to her face, I took great pains in making sure every cranny was clean, her eyes, her ears, and those lovely lips.

"He brought death to us, but I will deliver a fate ten times worse."

I rushed through washing her chest and her stomach, growing nauseous at her protruding ribs and her stomach that dipped lower than her once-luscious hipbones.

"He is darkness, but I will end him with light and sacrifice."

As I finished up, I knew she would appreciate being clean when she woke up. After grabbing a similar white dress that was laid out, I crumpled it up into a circle that would go over her head.

Her eyes were open, looking at me.

"Colby."

Panic rushed into her glassy blue eyes as she stared at me. Her lips were the first to quiver before the vibrations went throughout her body into an almost seizure-like motion.

"He's in me. He hates you. Says you don't love me."

Then the convulsions started— with piercing screams that I'd never heard from my mate and didn't want to ever again.

"Malynn!" I yelled out, my voice barely reaching a volume that was louder than Colby.

Malynn came in, making sure the curtain was closed behind her. She reached for a needle, and, with her knee on Colby's arm to stabilize her, stuck it into the tube in her arm and then released her.

The result was almost immediate.

The shaking and the screaming stopped as she was pulled under the tide of release.

Yet her eyes were still fixed on me. And all I could think of was that somewhere that bastard was killing her from the inside out and telling her all the while that I didn't love her.

If I wasn't going to be with her forever—at least she would know that I love her.

"Minha Querida, know that I love you with everything I am. I love you now and will love you into the beyond. No matter if it is here or in Paraiso, I will wait on you and love you every second until you come back to me."

Her eyes rolled back in her head, and she passed out again. There was no telling if my words sunk in or if they were lost in her drowning.

Slumping over on my side, I lay beside Colby. Malynn finished dressing her and sang some song that I could only equate with longing filled with words I didn't know but could comprehend so well.

There was nothing but lament and revenge in my heart. Sometimes, I thought that the vengefulness might be overruling the other. I couldn't let that happen.

Sanctum wouldn't take away the love I had in my heart. It was the only thing that separated me from him.

My love for her.

"Eidolon, I have seen your choice," Malynn whispered, checking Colby's vitals with what looked like rudimentary tools. She didn't meet my eyes. "I understand, but she will not. It will take years before she fully forgives you. Longer than that to forget. There are other choices."

Once again, I took advantage of my position in this place and among these people. "You will not tell a living soul about my choice. You will do your best to take care of my mate no matter where I am—if my heart is beating or not. Are we clear?"

I denied my baser instincts to say those things to her in such a manner, but she had to know the level of responsibility that I was giving to someone I'd met just days before.

There was no greater duty she could hold in my eyes than to be the protector and soother of my mate when—when I could not be.

"I understand, Eidolon. I won't let you down. I will be with her until my dying breath."

The thing was—there wasn't a choice at all. I couldn't kill Sanctum. Even if I could, it wouldn't solve our race's problem. There would be another Eidolon after me and another Sanctum after him.

It would continue until we learned our lesson.

Until we learned how to unite and function together.

Until the Eidolon rose to his responsibility.

Every group of people needed a martyr, right?

CHAPTER TWENTY-TWO
Collin

ARI'S HANDS WERE AROUND THE BARREL THAT WAS MY torso and she was using what puny strength she had for holding me back. I let her only because her ego was so fragile and she kind of scared me when it was compromised.

She strained to talk while stopping me. "You won't stop him. Whatever he's made up his mind to do—you can't stop him. He will just flash away and do it without us. We have a big enough war without creating new ones within ourselves."

I frowned down at her for acting silly. Saying big words while her tiny form was trying to hold me back was funny. The only reason I was letting her was because I would hurt her if I ran her over.

Except she wasn't being silly at all. She was dead on, and I knew it.

"He's being too generic. He's not saying what he means. I need to at least know what he means."

"Why?"

LILA FELIX

"So I can know how to stop him." I rolled my eyes at her. I didn't think I had ever done that before.

She pushed against my chest a little harder, surprising me. "And you think he will because you barge in there demanding that he say it? And even if he does, can we really stop him? I know he doesn't know what he's doing as the Eidolon. He seems to put out fires instead of having a solid plan of attack.

"But as Theo, Colby's mate, there was no guessing. He knew what she wanted and needed and he would stop at nothing to get the task completed for her. He once had me flash to Hawaii to get some Hibiscus flowers because she had a project but couldn't find one to show. He cashed in all of his savings bonds before her birthday to buy her a ring that she threw back at him, telling him that it was over. There was no length he wouldn't go to in order to do what she needs—nothing—including…"

"No. Don't say it. Damn it all. Don't say it."

I thrust my fingers into my hair, pulling it by the roots, hoping it would help me with the buried aggravation that I wouldn't be able to let out in front of Theo. "I know. Haven't you seen him since he came back this time? It was different. He didn't talk about the people in the Fray. There was no muscle soreness or disorientation like before. He's pensive and always looking to the sky in silence. And it's not because of Colby. I know him. Grinding his jaw or pumping his fists open and closed—that's for his hurting mate. The staring into space—the longing looks to the wide open—something else happened there that he's not telling us. I don't have powers like you all, but I know what I'm seeing."

"He will tell us. He's our friend."

She thumped her head against my chest in aggravation—or in giving up on me. "There are some things that are too painful even for friends. There are some burdens we have to carry alone. I think this is one of them for Theo. And as his friends, we have to respect that."

I turned my head to rest a cheek on the top of her head. I didn't like this part of it. I didn't like that he had to do anything alone.

That was what killed the last Eidolon—going at it alone—hiding himself and his family away from everyone instead of facing what was in front of him.

He even hid from his mate—staying longer and longer in the Fray to escape what his life had become—a shadow of what the Almighty meant for it to be.

"Come on. Let's check in with the teams. They have to have seen something by now."

"Ari..." I stopped her with my hand on her waist. She stopped and looked at me in question. We had been a little distant in the past days, handling everything and mostly just surviving. But seeing Theo long to say things to Colby that he might never get a chance to say made me more aware of the same thing happening to me. We didn't know what was going to happen when and if we ever found Pema.

And we probably wouldn't until it was too late.

So, I had to use up every second we got.

"I love you, Ari. I didn't think I'd ever find you—I didn't think I'd ever find a mate."

She rolled her eyes dramatically and lifted up on her tiptoes to kiss me quick and hard. "Don't get ahead of yourself, Viking. I found you. And I love you back infinity squared."

CHAPTER TWENTY-THREE
Theo

I LEFT COLBY TO REST IN THE MIDDLE OF THE NIGHT. Most of the Clandestine were taking shifts sleeping so that when Sanctum showed himself, we would all be ready. The desert was still. I couldn't hear a lick of wind outside. The same was true inside. Everyone was running on empty, but running like hell in spite of it.

"Any news?" I asked. I had felt something like static when I was lying next to Colby but ignored it. Maybe they were on to something.

"None," Collin answered.

An unexpected gust of wind blew the tent's flaps open, and Regina filled the empty space in an instant. She was out of breath with her hands on her knees, trying to steady herself. "I found them. Our team broke apart to search the area because we'd seen some red streaks in the sky. I found them. Both of them. I found the bastard."

A smile grew on her face. I wasn't the only one seeking revenge.

"Where?" I demanded.

"Easter Island. There's a hut there. He keeps going in and out of there, flashing. He must know we are near. I think he's flashing from there to Scotland. He's checking out that shadow thing of yours. It worked. I bet he didn't think we'd be on the other end. I bet he thinks she's safe."

Just as I'd pictured the island in my mind, Omar appeared.

"It worked, Eidolon. He's in Scotland. He's near the shadow. I think I saw him talking to it. Come quickly."

A smile tugged at one side of my face. "I don't need him. I need the woman. I'm going to Easter Island."

Regina flashed first. As soon as I'd pinpointed her location, I flashed to her, almost knocking her over.

"It's there. The shack. See how he comes and goes? He's afraid."

There was a three to four-minute span between him leaving and coming back. Three minutes was all I had to take his mate like he had taken mine. It was our only chance to get him to stop hurting Colby.

"Wait, Theo. There's some kind of protection around the shack. I tried to get near it, but it was like hitting a wall. You can see the sheen of it if you look close enough."

I froze in place. How would I get through that? But if he had that power, then I had something in my Eidolon arsenal to combat it. "I can get through it. We just have to time it correctly."

She nodded, and we waited for him to flash back. Shadows moved within the tiny house by the light of the moon, so bright without being blocked by buildings.

Then, like clockwork, he flashed out of there, leaving a wake-like flash around the place.

I ran to the building and remembered how I'd put my face through the window at my apartment. If there was a time to use that weird gift, now was it. Testing it with my pointer finger, I focused on what was beyond the wake. It worked. I soon stuck my whole hand in. With not much time left, I passed through the barrier and opened the door.

Pema was crouched just inside, her hands around her stomach.

"Pema, come with me. Don't fight this. I don't want to hurt you."

But I'd spoken too soon. In this state, Pema couldn't have fought off an ant from biting her arm. She was nothing but a skeleton like Colby, but there was a dodgeball-sized swell under her baggy dress. Her hair had grown a little, but there were spots on the top and the middle that were bare.

He was killing them both.

"Theo. He's killing us," she said and then fainted right into my arms.

When I flashed into the tent with Pema, the rest of the people gathered were as confused as I was about how to proceed and what to do with her. On the one hand, she was Sanctum's mate or breeding buddy. She carried the spawn of one who we would rather not exist at all.

We certainly didn't want him creating more little bastards to run around wreaking havoc.

But on the other hand, and I realized this more and more as I held her pitiful form, was that she was a female Lucent at the core. She was one of our people. The only difference between her and the others was that she had made a really lousy choice.

We couldn't just let him kill her.

"I know," I said to Collin as he stepped forward to take her from my arms.

"She is a descendent of the last Eidolon. She will be treated as such, regardless of her— situation."

I nodded. "I knew you would, Collin. You are honorable to a fault."

He chuckled. "It is not without a second thought of leaving her stranded somewhere to suffer. Believe me. Not that honorable."

It was actually the very definition of honorable—wanting to do something wrong but doing the right thing anyway.

Ari walked with him down the hallway to

put Pema in their room for the night, I assumed.

The thing was—I now had to face my brother alone.

CHAPTER TWENTY-FOUR
Sanctum

THE DAMNED SHADOW WAS JUST THAT—A SHADOW.

"What in the hell, Theodore?"

I was off my game—that much was for sure.

Picturing the shack in my head, I flashed back to check on the imp.

But she was nowhere to be found.

"Damn you, Pema! Where did you go?"

But my lightning protection remained around the cabin. She couldn't have passed through it. She was too weak.

There was only one who could've broken through it.

"Theodore. Oh, brother, what have you done?"

CHAPTER TWENTY-FIVE
Theo

I MADE HIM WAIT TWO DAYS. THE WOMEN WHO WERE once the Synod kept tabs on him as he paced and threw fits by the shack and in Scotland. Once he knew that what he saw was my shadow and not me, he approached it. Upon my command, it vanished into thin air.

Pema was awake, but barely. Her breathing was shallow, and I had to make the decision on whether or not to give her nutrients.

My mind wanted me to treat her like the traitor she was, but the part of me that was Eidolon wouldn't have a Lucent woman treated that way, even though he'd treated my mate that way.

I made my rounds, checking in on both of them. Pema hadn't spoken yet, so when I heard a whisper leave her mouth, I paid attention.

"What did you say? And choose your words carefully. You are still a traitor in our eyes." I sounded downright stupid trying to be badass. It never had worked for me.

"Take this off me. Only you…"

Her voice ran dry. I had no idea what she was talking about.

"This," she croaked out, scratching at her neck. There was a deep red mark around her neck, extending down into the collar of her dress.

"Collin, come see," I said, wanting some kind of witness. I was still a gentleman. In spite of who she was, it didn't change my honor.

With my finger hooked under her chin, I turned her head right and left, inspecting what looked like burns. The surface of her skin had fresh scratches that were bleeding and scabbed over.

"What the hell is this?" I asked her.

"A piece of her—of piece of you."

Pressing a finger to the line around her neck, I felt something inside. I traced the protrusion around until, with my throat constricting, I realized what was going on.

"He buried something in your neck?"

She nodded but turned to her left, no longer wishing to look at me. She had to be ashamed, and her guilt was almost palpable in the air.

"Collin, we are going to need Malynn for this one."

Collin left the room and I sat back on my heels, not wanting to think about how he did that to her and what she had been promised in return.

Malynn and Collin came back in a good while

later. While she examined Pema, Collin and I went back to visit Colby. A million thoughts skidded through my mind as we walked the short distance.

Not only had Pema allowed Sanctum to impregnate her, but she also had something similar to Colby. Now, it was killing them both.

And the bastard had put something under her skin. There was just no telling what he had thought to do, but Malynn, I was sure, would get it out of her fast.

I squinted, not believing my eyes when I walked into Colby's room. There wasn't that much of a marked difference, but there was some—and at that point, progress was progress.

"Is it wishful thinking or does she look a little less pale today?"

Collin looked over my shoulder. "You are right. She is a little less pale."

Collin walked out of the room while I knelt next to Colby and thanked the Almighty for that small favor. I didn't know how it happened, but a small reprieve was all I needed to continue to hope that all of this would work out—that my plan would be fulfilled and she would be okay.

"Eidolon, I think you need to see this." Malynn flitted in and out, in a hurry to get back to what she'd found.

"I'm coming." I placed a chaste kiss on Colby's lips and left her again.

When I got back to Pema's room, there was

a full-on surgical table set up with Pema as the patient, complete with a hospital gown.

"Where in the hell did you get all of this?" I asked, looking at the equipment while trying not to shake in anger that this stuff was not used on my mate.

Malynn paled. "I had to, Eidolon. This was surgery, not like Colby. I did flash to a hospital to get the medicines for Colby, but I needed sterile conditions to do what I needed to here."

The place smelled like disinfectant and iodine. Bloody tools sat on a metal side table. Pema was out cold with bandages covering her neck.

"What was it? Was there something in there?"

"Wait—let me get something to hold it." She looked at the metal table and covered her mouth while making a gagging sound.

She came back in with a long metal rod that looked like a fire poker, maneuvering it around before pulling it up to reveal what was buried in the last Eidolon's ancestor. "I gave her a local anesthetic, but she kind of passed out when she saw the blood. She will heal, but she needs food and water. She's dehydrated and malnourished. She will always bear the scar of her decisions in more ways than one."

"Is it a necklace?"

Malynn shuddered as she looked at the thing. The chain was heavy and thick, the pendant at the bottom was oval and egg-shaped.

"I think there's something inside it, Eidolon. My mind pictured him putting something inside this egg thing when I touched it. But it made me so sick that I threw it down." Tears came to her eyes, and her hand shook as she continued to hold up the offending piece of jewelry. "He is—he is so completely evil, Theo. I know that Colby had dreams of fixing him—of somehow restoring him to your brother again. She was so worried that you would mourn the loss of your brother even more after all of this was over." She looked at him with her jaws clenched. "He cannot be saved. He is the root of all evil, and there is no good intention in him. Just the thought of him makes me sour."

My eyes went back to the necklace. If there was something inside of it, then we needed to find out what it was.

"Let me try," I offered, holding my hand out.

"Eidolon, you cannot. Your gift—you are too pure—too good to even stand in the same room as whatever conjuring he has placed on this object. Let my father touch it, or Collin, or anyone."

I huffed out my rebuttal and ignored her pleading. If I was as pure as she had said, then it shouldn't affect me.

"Let me try," I said, reaching for it. As soon as I touched the cold metal, though it had just come from Pema's body, a punch of gut-wrenching pain hit my torso, as though it had reached into me and was fisting my heart.

"Stop, Eidolon, it will kill you. That kind of power is too evil."

I heard her, but at the same time, the evil powered me on. I had to get through it in order to stop the curse. "No. I won't stop until I get to it."

I had to close my eyes and concentrate on the task at hand. As I used my fingernails to dig into the carvings on the shell of the egg pendant, I was desperate to find a way in. Never in my life had I experienced a panic attack, but while working to find the opening, my breaths were taken from me and my skin felt like worms were crawling underneath the surface. The pain in my chest radiated down to my stomach and up to my head, pounding like having a chorus of seven migraines at once.

"There." I finally found the crease in the pendant and cracked it open. Inside were strings of something, singed and rotten. The smell that came forth from that tiny pendant was more pungent than a thousand sewers doused with sulphur.

"What is it?" I asked aloud. I turned to her, seeking an answer when I realized we'd been joined by Eliza, Regina, Omar, and Collin. Ari came in just as I spoke.

"Oh, crap on a cracker, that smells like an alligator curled up, died, and decayed right in the middle of someone's ass crack."

Collin shut his eyes and slammed his lips together before calmly saying, "Ari, I don't think this is the time for your graphic explanations."

She shrugged. "You're right, I guess. That shit says it all by the smell. And by the way, I'm a graphic kind of girl. Get over it."

I held the charred, straw-like contents in my palms and rushed outside before everyone in the tents began throwing up like I wanted to. Pushing back the gagging, I broke through the tent's entrance. For once, I welcomed the dry, desert air.

"Let me see what's in it." Malynn was crouching next to where I'd collapsed from the relief of not having to be cooped up with that horrid scent.

"Don't touch it. It's killing me to hold it. I don't want it to hurt you any more than it already has. Just look and cover your mouth and nose."

She pulled up the scarf she already wore and covered most of her face. I tried to move the contents around so she could get a good look, but it still resembled nothing that I would expect—more like spider webs in a clump.

I spat. "Wait... that son of a..."

Collin was behind me again, looking over at the scene. There was something about his presence; I always knew when he was near. "Eidolon, that is hair. It is a clump of hair."

I knew that already, but hearing Collin

confirm the fact made me even angrier. I tested the limits of its power by smashing the contents between my palms and rolling it back and forth, trying to separate what seemed like two different textures.

"There are two clumps of hair, twisted together. Then burned?"

"No," Malynn answered. She had gotten one of the blades from Pema's surgery and was now prodding the hair. "They were put in and then have become burned from the power of the spell or magic that was infused into this object. Wait..." She closed her eyes and crouched into a ball, holding her head in her hands. "It is Rebekkah's necklace. No, just the pendant. The pendant belongs to the last Prophetess. He stole it from her when he..." She trailed off, not wanting to say that he had stolen the pendant from Rebekkah when he murdered her in cold blood.

"Whose hair is it and why was it inside her neck?"

"It doesn't matter. We need to bind this magic. We have to seal it in something pure."

Omar stepped forward, blocking the sun from my eyes. "I have an idea."

CHAPTER TWENTY-SIX
Sanctum

I SAT AT THE TOP OF THE EMPIRE STATE BUILDING, WAITING and watching. It was nearly three o'clock in the morning, but New York City thought it was broad daylight, the way they were still in full swing.

Theodore had stolen her from me—stolen them from me.

Pema was gone despite my best efforts to save her. I hadn't realized when I bound the fate of Pema to Colby that carrying my fetus would kill her slowly—and kill Colby in the process.

I'd only meant to hurt both of them long enough for Theo to relent.

The real Sanctum, the ruler of all things evil, called to me from the depths of hell. The inside of my temples burned and forced me to recognize his calling. I had free reign on this Earth. Even if he came up here, he couldn't stop me from running—or flashing as it was.

Just like the Synod, the devil had no real power. He was bound to Hell, forced to rely on demons and minions like me to do his dirty work.

All of his power was in the minds of those he carried dominion over.

And if they would stop giving him power in their minds, he would have none.

I had felt every tug of skin and bone as someone cut out my connection to Pema. But they could remove it all they wanted to. I was already in Colby's head, and she was sealed to Pema and my spawn's lives just like Colby and Theo were bound.

If my child died, so would Colby.

If Pema died, so would Colby.

I cursed the stars and thought about my options, which were few. The thought of bargaining with Theodore came to mind. I spat onto the patrons below me. If I had my way, those pesky humans wouldn't even exist. They would all die away, and the Lucents would rule the world.

Well, most of the Lucents.

The plans I'd had and the reasoning for my war crumbled beneath my fingers and floated on the air.

There was nothing left for me to fight for except the unborn child in Pema's womb. She was probably crying to them and telling them everything that I should've never told her in the first place.

"A little bargaining for the blonde Barbie's

life should do the trick."

And with that, I flashed back to Easter Island and awaited the man I hated most in the world—my brother.

CHAPTER TWENTY-SEVEN
Theo

"I AM THE BIGGEST IDIOT ON THE PLANET—WE ARE THE biggest idiots on the planet," Malynn screamed at the top of her lungs the next night as we gathered silently in the main room. Colby had not progressed since the day I'd found her less pale, and Pema had still not woken from her post-surgery faint.

Malynn did an ultrasound and found that while the child was still small for the gestational timetable, that it was vital and very much alive.

"Malynn, you speak out of turn," Omar fussed at her, but I agreed a little.

"Fine, I can be punished later. Theodore, when I was braiding Colby's hair for her visit to the Synod, there was a piece of her hair that was way shorter than the rest.

"Holy shit." It all fit together, with that one sentence. "Wait, how in the hell did he get her hair?"

Everyone slinked away at my question.

Malynn continued, "So that's the skin. It wasn't skin—it was hair. He took some of her hair and somehow bound himself to her. That's how he controls her body—how he manipulates her mind—all of it. But why in the holy hell would it be in her..." She made a round motion around her neck.

"If that's true, then whose hair is the other? It's too long to be Pema's."

My stomach turned sour. "It's his. It is Sanctum's hair mixed with my mate's." My words were monotone and unbelievably calm for what I'd just discovered. I didn't know why I'd expected anything less.

What I hadn't told a living soul was that this wasn't the first time my brother had expressed some interest in Colby. He had probably been in love with her as long as I had, or at least the closest thing to affection a bastard like him could feel.

I didn't have any proof; it was just one of those things that I knew by instinct.

The only reason I knew nothing had happened when the two of them were together was because I trusted Colby with everything in me.

And she thought he was icky.

Ari was stewing, sitting cross-legged on the floor. "So, if this was their link or whatever, then if we break it, Colby should be good, right?"

We all looked to Malynn, but judging from her downward stare, it wasn't anything we wanted to hear.

"Malynn?"

"Eidolon, I'm not sure how to say this. The hair was just his gateway? Door? I'm not sure how to explain it, but once he's in, he is the only one who can remove himself from her. And even if he does, at this point, I'm not sure either one will recover."

"What? Are you telling me that he's in there permanently? Even if we destroy this weird voodoo thing he's cooked up, Colby won't be spared? Is that what you are telling me?" I slammed my fists down on the table in front of me, unwilling to accept her words at face value. It couldn't be true. This wasn't the way it was supposed to work. I was supposed to figure all of this shit out and fix it.

Because if I couldn't fix what was happening to my own mate, then how in the hell was I fit to do anything the Almighty asked of me?

"I'm sorry, Eidolon. Yes, that's what I'm telling you. He will have to be the one to end this."

I stood and looked at everyone in the room. Though their efforts had been valiant, there was nothing else they could do for me—for us.

So, instead of guerilla tactics, I went for the throat. Taking out my phone, I dialed my brother.

He answered on the first ring of course. "Theodore. I assumed you would be calling." His words said that, but his tone said something else altogether. He was scared and he should be.

"I have your mate—or your breeding buddy—whichever you prefer. We cut out the necklace you buried in her. By the way, that was weird. I didn't know you were so kinky. Anyway, we have her and your spawn. I will give her back to you and you can have Rosemary's baby back. All you have to do is get out of my mate's head."

He clicked his tongue over the phone. I'd never heard a nastier sound.

"You know what? I'm not sure that's going to work for me." I heard rustling and wondered where he was so I could tear him apart limb from limb. "How about I give you a little option since you are clearly the desperate one in this situation? How about you bring me to Paraiso, since apparently the Synod isn't going to do their job—again—and then I can resume my prior plan? If not, I will kill Colby in the next—say—hour? How does that feel, Theo? To know that she will be ripped from you in sixty minutes? Hurts, doesn't it? Especially since all this time, I've been feeding her lies about how you are no longer interested in her as your mate and how she should've never been your mate in the first place."

"That's not true," I growled into the phone.

I heard the sound of fabric, and I knew my brother well enough to know he was shrugging. He didn't give a damn. "You know, it doesn't matter what is true and false at this point.

Remember how the Synod took power over the Lucent? It's the loudest voice that solidifies our beliefs. And right now, I'm the loudest damned thing in Colby's world because I am the only thing in her world. You don't matter anymore. I've all but convinced her that you've abandoned her for your precious duties.

"I'll repeat myself if you missed some of that. I know you're a little slow. Bring me to the army of the Almighty, and I will let her live. She won't love you anymore and she won't want to be your mate, but at least she will be alive. Isn't that the sacrifice all you hero types want to make in the end?"

I stayed silent. He and I listened to the echo of each other's breathing for a while, absorbing this long overdue conversation.

"There is another option, brother." I spat the word, hating, again, that he was my family.

"No, that's where you're wrong."

"It isn't my option. It isn't yours either. But yes, in the end, I think it will be the only way to solve all of this. In fact, I'd already made up my mind before calling you. I just wanted to give you one more chance to end all of this yourself."

He cackled on the other line.

"Meet me in person. I'm sick to death of fighting a war with you from afar."

"In Portugal—where it all started—at the house of Xoana. Give me three hours."

His answer was swift. "Done."

CHAPTER TWENTY-EIGHT
Theo

MANY TIMES, MORE THAN I COULD COUNT, I'D BEEN ON a one-way street in terms of expressing my love to Colby.

This time, she really wouldn't be able to say anything back to me.

And this time, I thought maybe I was okay with it.

"Colby, Querida, I think somewhere deep down you can hear me. You're going to wake up soon—sooner than you think. Sanctum is going to be out of your head and out of our lives. I think you're going to have to help take care of Pema. I know you hate her, but she will have no one else in the world and a tiny Torrent on her hands. I don't know when the baby will be claimed for the other side, but it will be eventually, so don't get attached."

I didn't know why I expected her to get up and make a smartass remark back to me, but I did.

"Ari and Malynn are going to be here when you wake up. They will explain some things,

I hope. But there are some promises I'm not going to be able to keep. I will not be able to place my hand on the swell of your belly when you are having our child—because there will never be a child. I won't get a peach cobbler belly like my dad and live to see how beautiful you will be with gray hair. But I can make some new promises. You will find a new mate and you will have children. Malynn has seen it."

Malynn attempted to interrupt, but she quickly closed her mouth. We were surrounded by Ari, Collin, and all the others who had become more than friends, more like family.

"One day, I will see you again—I can promise that. You won't be mine anymore, but you will be happy and living the life you were meant to live. When we were kids, there were no lengths I wouldn't go to give you what you deserved. So many things have changed between us. We went from friends to lovers, back to friends, and then back to lovers. But one thing hasn't changed. I will still give up everything for you. I always have, and I always will. I've given Ari a list of the things that you like and where she can get them. If you need a Slush Puppie, she knows the locations. I know you think I gave her that list for when I was in the Fray, but I had already thought way beyond that tiny time frame. There are some other things in place for you. I have a house purchased in Louisiana. My parents have the location. That's for you and your—mate when you find him. Malynn will be by your side from now on. I don't want anything to happen to you, and you will still be considered the mate of the Eidolon even though..."

I looked up at Malynn, who confirmed my promise with a nod.

"The best thing about all this is that I was made an offer by the Almighty. It happened the last time I was there. He has promised that if I give up everything, there are two things that will happen—one, Sanctum will be gone. Our creator is a creator of balance. And if there is no Eidolon, then there is no Sanctum. I have fulfilled my duty by the Almighty, and there will never be another Eidolon in the future. There won't need to be. The Fray will disappear with me. I think it was made to test us somehow. I don't really know. It's one of many questions I have for the big guy when I get up there. Second, my precious mate, is that you will no longer remember any of this. You will remember me from our childhood, but nothing past the night that you ended it with me. You won't remember all of these trials. You won't remember the day we were sealed. It will all be gone. It will all be forgotten."

Ari and Collin gasped. I thought they had an inkling about what would eventually have to happen, but they didn't want to face it.

I had no choice now but to face it.

With one last kiss to her temple, I told Colby goodbye.

CHAPTER TWENTY-NINE
Sanctum

HE WAS STALLING. I DIDN'T FARE WELL WITH STALLING, especially when I felt like I was unprotected and unprepared for something. In my mind, I had the upper hand. Theo's mate was clearly on the brink of death, and I was the cause of it.

There was nothing he could do. He had to submit to what I wanted or else she would die.

Pema would die.

And I knew that, unlike me, Theo wouldn't be worth anything once Colby died.

I hadn't even noticed that he flashed in until I heard his voice. "Torrent, you look surprised to see me. Isn't this where we decided to meet?"

"It is. You have no wake. You simply surprised me."

Theo took a seat on the couch like this was some informal meeting. "I have more surprises for you. Just you wait."

I shot him my devious smile, but inside, I was shaking beyond control. I knew so much more than he did about our world and what our powers were used for, but somehow, his confidence and ease at the situation disturbed me.

"But first," he went on, "I have some questions. I mean, this is all about to end, so I'd like to go on about my business with at least some answers."

"Okay..." I shook my head. Everything was foggy and my head was cloudy.

"So, when did you decide to go all *Hellboy* on us?"

I looked outside at Xoana's gardens. What once was beautiful was now withered. Trees were dried out and falling—hollowed out. Leaves were brown and crisp. Even the grass had decided to no longer grow.

"What happened out there?"

He looked outside, but again, was completely at ease, which drove me nuts.

"Out there? Oh, I think He told me something about that. You see, when Colby and I were sealed here, the land of Xoana recognized us as the Eidolon couple. But when Colby got sick—I mean, when you made her sick—the land of Xoana started to mourn. This is the result."

"That doesn't make sense," I murmured.

"Let's get back to the question, shall we?"

I heard a swish of air and turned to find Ari and Collin had joined us. "Do we need witnesses?" I smiled.

"I have bigger witnesses than these two. But no, they are here for my sake. To make sure everything goes as planned. It's just for my peace of mind. So…" he pushed. "*Hellboy*?"

He acted like we were on some kind of timetable. To him, I guessed we were. He had a mate at home who was dying a slow and painful death.

"I think I've always known I was different. You were Mom and Dad's golden child. There wasn't really a place for someone who felt and acted differently. I was the outcast. And then there was Colby."

He didn't flinch like I hoped he might. But Ari and her new man did. Theo was such a good secret keeper. Even his keeping of that secret was a shock to me.

"Really? That's it? Mom and Dad, in your perspective, didn't love you as much as they did me, and you couldn't have Colby, so you decided to devote your life to the devil and give up your soul? Damn, most kids get a tattoo or start wearing black. You may have wanted to try guy-liner before going that far. I heard it helps."

I squinted at him. His legs were crossed and he was laid back in the chair like a mafia boss. Today, more than any day I'd seen him of late, he looked like Theo. He was wearing one of those button-down shirts with gray pants, like he was dressed up.

Hopefully, this was his funeral attire as well.

"It doesn't matter the reason, Theodore. And

I'm tired of the questions. Are you ready to go or not? Your girl is on the edge, and I'm about to kick her right off."

"What about Pema? What about your tiny little emo child waiting to be born?"

Tiny little emo kid—his sarcasm was getting better.

"It doesn't matter anymore. It won't save me. Nothing will save me, Theodore. It's too late."

CHAPTER THIRTY
Theo

HE WAS WRONG. MY BROTHER WAS WRONG. I SMILED TO myself because I knew now, even more than I did before, that I was right. In one swoop, I could save us all. I could save myself from a lifetime of leaving Colby over and over by going to the Fray, knowing that she would spend her life half in pain and half in happiness.

I could save myself from the guilt all of that caused.

I would save Colby from living that life. She would have a mate she could count on all the time, not just when it was convenient for him. She would have children and not have to worry about the times when I would leave and make her, temporarily, a single mother.

She would have a stable, stress-free life.

And now, looking at my brother, and that twinge of regret I could see in his face, I knew that my choice would ultimately save him too. Because once he was left with no powers, he would be useless to the real enemy. He would be cast aside and forgotten.

"Do you love that female, brother?" I asked the question in earnest.

"I am incapable of love." He looked away.

"I don't think that's true. It was only too easy to catch Pema on Easter Island, and such an obvious place. You were obsessed with that place when we were kids. And if I can move through things, so can you, so you already knew I could get to your little short-haired female. You know what I think? I think you wanted me to find her and save her. I think you were scared that she wouldn't make it, and you knew we would take care of her."

His eyebrow cocked but he said nothing. So telling.

"That's okay, brother. There's a painless way to end all of this. Come with me. It will soon be done."

He followed me with a lot less fight than I thought he'd give. In fact, he gave no fight at all. We walked through the gardens, and as we did, they came back to life under my feet. The grass turned to green and stood at attention. The flowers perked up and went into full bloom. The bushes sprouted leaves and took their former shapes.

I walked all the way out to Rebekkah's grave—the grave where I realized such a long time ago that in order for things to be okay, that a sacrifice must be made.

Rebekkah had made her sacrifice in order to

put things in motion.

Collin had made his sacrifice of his position to help me.

Ari had sacrificed her life, along with my mate, in order to support me.

But now it was my turn.

"After I'm gone, please go to our parents. You'll have to go old school, I'm afraid. Tell them everything so that when Colby wakes up, they will be in the know."

He looked confused and sputtered something akin to 'What the hell?'

"Ari, you know what to do. Flash to Colby as soon as I'm gone. I don't want her to wake up alone. Also, watch those naked shower shenanigans, Collin will get jealous."

Ari began to cry, so I pulled her in for the hug I'd intended to give her anyway. She'd never underestimated how much Colby needed her. Above all others, other than Colby, I was grateful to her.

"I cannot tell you how incredibly thankful I am that you were here with us through this all. I know you won't leave her alone for too long. Make sure she finds that mate. Make sure he's up to my standards, okay? Make sure he's good enough for her."

She nodded and then passed her tears onto Collin's shirt.

"What the hell is happening, Theo?"

I had already spoken my peace to Collin in

the middle of the night. He would need to be Ari's strong pillar so that she could be Colby's, so we got all the sappy stuff out of the way.

"I'm going to set you free, brother. You became who you are out of hatred, greed, and jealousy. And I'm going to give you your life back out of love. This will be the end of the Eidolon comings. The Lucents won't need a leader after me. I believe we have learned our lesson well."

"Theo, there has to be another way," Ari pleaded one last time.

"There isn't, Ari. Don't tell her that I love her. Don't even mention my name—trust me—she won't."

And there, in the gardens of the female, Xoana, who started it all, who stood face to face with the Almighty and cursed the life she was doomed to live, I called on the Almighty, as he had told me to do when I was ready, and gave it all up for those I loved. I would come face to face with the Almighty Himself, not for my own blessing, but for my love and my friends.

Finally, finally, I had become the leader I was born to be.

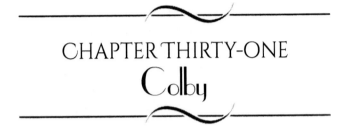

CHAPTER THIRTY-ONE
Colby

I WOKE UP IN MY BED. ARI WAS SLEEPING ON THE FLOOR next to me. "Get up, you ass. Why are you on the floor?" I kicked at her.

She woke up, startled. "You're awake?"

"Duh," I said, staring back.

"Are you hungry?" she asked. She knew better. I didn't really get hungry. I liked to stay thin so I could flash easily. The girl wasn't really awake yet.

"Actually, I am a little. I feel like I've lost a ton of weight."

"Colby, you were out for a long time. You've been—in—a—coma for a couple of months. We didn't know if we'd get you back or not."

I tried to get up to look in the mirror, but I found my legs didn't want to cooperate. "No joke? What happened to me?"

She got up and picked up her blankets. "We don't know. You flashed back after going to Rebekkah's funeral. When you went to sleep, you never woke up again. We were supposed to go on vacation, but you punked out and slept for like two months."

Tears welled in my eyes, remembering the funeral, but the memories were faded and fuzzy, like patches were missing. "I must've been sick or something even then. I can barely remember anyone who was there. Did Theo come to the funeral?"

Ari went to the door and opened it. "I've got to go pee. But don't you remember? The jerk stopped e-mailing you. Said he had finally given up on you. He even had the nerve to have me give you the message. What an asshole."

When her voice tripped over the last sentence, she said something about her throat being dry and rushed to the bathroom.

I finally convinced my legs to work, but I had to hold on to pieces of furniture in my room in order to stand up straight. "I need a dress. I smell like Shrek or something."

"You kind of do," Ari answered, walking back in. "Here, let me help you. Malynn is coming over later."

"Who?"

She cleared her throat. "Malynn. She was your nurse while you were out, and we kind of became friends. She'll want to check you out but also, she's nice. Give her a chance."

"Oooo… kay…" I answered. While her back was turned, I pinched myself to make sure this wasn't one of my freaky dreams.

She handed me a green maxi dress and

pushed me to take a shower, but she came into the bathroom with me.

"I can take a shower myself, Ari. What the hell are you doing? You're going to take a shower with me? Get a grip."

She huffed out a laugh that was completely fake. "No. Don't be stupid, Colby."

We met Malynn, who was pretty funny and had a strange accent. She and Ari got along well, and she had killer hair.

"Everything looks okay," she said after checking my blood pressure and oxygen. I guessed she was also some kind of home health nurse. I didn't really ask questions.

"Where's my mom?"

Ari shrugged. "Shopping or working, probably, not sure."

A few weeks passed, and I still felt like I had just woken up the first day. I had gained some weight since Malynn convinced me that I was way underweight. She made me promise to eat a little more and though I didn't want to admit it, I had more energy when I did.

I answered some e-mails and picked up some new jobs for the next month. I needed to get back to work and back to life.

Ari stayed close, which was weird for her.

"Have you heard from Sway?" I asked one day while she was hanging around my house—again.

"Nope. She's being weird. Not talking to us

again."

She didn't look at me when she spoke lately. And that wasn't all. My mom avoided me at all costs. There was no word from Theo in weeks. I knew that boy like the back of my hand—even when I made him leave me alone, he never really left me alone.

"Dude, I've gotten so skinny that I bet I don't even fit in that wedding dress anymore." I got up and went to the closet, determined to try it on. I loved that dress.

"Why are you even going to try it on? You'll just look stupid. Anyway, you got it made for him and he's not coming back."

She shoved the magazine she was not really reading back in her face.

"What do you mean he's not coming back? Did he come to see me when I was in that coma or whatever?"

"Fine. Just try it on." She changed the subject.

"I will."

I pulled out the dress. After taking off my clothes, I got it off the hanger and pulled it on.

But the damned thing didn't look the same.

And it was way bigger than I remembered. I hadn't lost that much weight. I just hadn't.

"What happened? This—what happened?"

There were stiches along the waist that didn't look like the others. It was like someone had added fabric to the back as well.

"You're so dramatic. Look in the mirror, Colby.

Nothing has changed."

I sidestepped while sticking my tongue out at her in the mirror. "What is that smell?" I pulled one of the sleeves up to my nose before falling to my knees. It started with the vision of myself in the mirror—in this very dress—except it was too small instead of too big.

"Colby, what's wrong?" Ari shouted to me, but her voice seemed so far away.

"Our hands," I muttered. "Our hands were joined in lightning."

She stood still behind me—our eyes fixed in the reflection.

"He took this dress off me. Damn it, Ari. Where is he? Is he there? That place he used to go?"

She stuttered for a bit until I twisted around and grabbed her with both of my hands on her face. "Damn you, Ari. Where did he go?"

I was screaming at Ari at the top of my lungs, frantic and desperate for her to tell me something that would validate the flooding of emotions and unconnected visions.

My mom burst through the door, alarmed at my screams. "What is happening in here?"

"You lied to me. You all effing lied to me. He's not gone. He's not gone. I can find him."

I slapped my hands over my ears and pushed all of my strength into the memories that were on the tips of my fingers. What I could remember was more than visual. It was the touch of Theo's hands on my hips. The way his breath tickled the back of my neck in the morning. The muscles along his spine that stretched and pulled with his shoulders so beautifully. His voice in the dark. My voice when it changed to speak to only him.

"I can't. Why can't I find him?" I pounded my fists on the ground in pure anger.

"Colby, look at me. Come on, girl. Calm down. Ari has gone to get Collin. You remember Collin?"

I swallowed against my anger and zeroed in on my mom's voice. "The Viking? She's bringing the Viking?"

"I'm here, Colby. And I never thought I'd relish you calling me that again. Come on, dear friend. Let's go sit down after you change, and I will explain everything. I don't even know how you remember, but this has to mean something."

They left my room and I sat on the edge of the bed, not yet willing to take off the dress that had sparked everything.

"Theo, where are you?" I allowed myself time to cry and slowly changed back into the regular dress. I took my time in hanging my wedding dress back up and carefully placing it back into the closet. My hand stayed on it for another five minutes, mourning the loss of so many memories.

In a daze, I went to the living room and

waited for an explanation. The depression phase had gone. In its place was anger and rage—mostly rage.

"Colby, we are not sure how this is even possible. What do you remember?"

Collin's voice had triggered even more memories to come forth, and they did so with a fury. I rattled them off as they came to me. The first time I pulled on that rope to ring his doorbell. Asking him if he could fly the helicopter while he was injured. In the cabin with Theo and him bringing me Slush Puppies. The chanting monks. The books in Belgium. And that was just the beginning.

But mostly, I remembered the lightning— the lightning that came from Theo as he flashed. The lightning that encircled our hands in joining light on the day of our sealing.

None of the lightning was forgotten.

"When he left..." Collin cleared his throat. "When he released himself of the powers and gave himself up to Paraiso, a bolt of lightning peeled down the clouds and bulleted to him. I'd never seen anything like it before, and I doubt I ever will again. It nearly blinded me. It was so brilliant. I saw him go. But all of this— all of this goes against the deal. Ari, did you call Torrent?"

Raw rage ballooned in my chest. "Torrent? You mean Sanctum. Don't call him!"

"Colby, so much changed when Theo

sacrificed himself. You got better, mostly because Sanctum's powers were based on Theo's powers and once they were gone—there was nothing else for Sanctum to have dominion over. There is no longer a Fray. Our people don't get lost anymore. The Synod is no more. They realized that we are better off when we govern ourselves. Torrent is back to human again. He is mated to Pema, and she's still pregnant. But you were supposed to forget. That was part of the deal. Hell, even I didn't know how we were going to keep up the charade, but we promised him. It was an impossible one, but a promise nonetheless. It would mean we would have to lie to you for the rest of our lives and yours— he never should've made us make the vow."

Ari was crying. She sat down and rested her face in her hands. Theo had given her a task that would plague her for the rest of her life. And she had taken it on, knowing it.

I didn't understand anything Ari was saying to me. There were some things I knew, but they were far away like the end of a rope that I couldn't quite reach.

Theo's voice flooded my mind. *Second, my precious mate, is that you will no longer remember any of this. You will remember me from our childhood and nothing past the night that you ended it with me. You won't remember all of these trials. You won't remember the day we were sealed. It will all be gone.*

It will all be forgotten.
I will still give up everything for you. I always have and I always will.

CHAPTER THIRTY-TWO
Theo

I THOUGHT THAT PARAISO WOULD ACTUALLY BE BORING. Even though I had been there, in my mind, it was still a white place with people in white gowns playing harps and singing their days away.

That wasn't Paraiso at all.

Paraiso was The Almighty's kingdom come. Yes, everyone was happy, but we still had our own lives to carry out. But life carried no stress. There was mourning and sorrow for those we couldn't be with anymore, but all beneath a veil of joy.

I had a home, like everyone else. There were pictures on the walls of those I loved, except Colby. My memories of her were only hung in my mind.

I got up from my chair and put down my book that day, hearing a distant sound that I didn't recognize.

Looking out the window, I saw nothing amiss.

I took one step backward and plunged down—falling—falling.

CHAPTER THIRTY-THREE
Colby

I SAT UP, DAYS LATER, GASPING FOR AIR. THIS WASN'T ANY different from the rest of my days. I seemed to wake up every day with a gasp and go to sleep every night whimpering.

I'd sent Ari back home. She and Collin had an apartment a few miles away, but I missed her presence near me.

Everything seemed robotic now.

It was better before, when I was stupid, when I didn't know which way was up.

Mostly, it was better when I didn't know that Theo was gone.

It was better to be ignorant.

I checked my e-mail and set up some more appointments to work. Working was the only thing keeping me halfway sane. In between appointments, my friends attempted to keep me busy. Their idea of busy was Netflix binges and karaoke of all things.

Collin knocked Journey out of the park.

But he wept like a little girl when we made him watch *Dawson's Creek*.

We all did.

Collin had gone to work—he'd passed the civil service exam and become a librarian when I was still out. Ari had to buy falsified documents from one of her special sources, but it was legit enough to get him a visa and permission to work in the country.

She had done the same for Malynn, but she had decided to enroll in online school and was living with my mother and me.

I hadn't contacted Theo's parents. I didn't know what they knew, and I couldn't bear to put the same look on their faces that I had born just a short time ago.

As I placed one of the emails into the virtual trash, I glanced over to that folder—the one where Theo's emails had always gone.

I turned the computer off before I could read one of them. I was still in the anger part of mourning. Yes, I missed him—missed him like a phantom limb. But I was also pissed. It wasn't supposed to end that way. We were supposed to end Sanctum and be free. He was the bad guy and that was how bad guys ended—the good guys made sure of it.

That wasn't our fairy tale. Fairy tales weren't real, and I was proof of it.

Mostly my anger was centered on Theo. He promised me things. He'd held my hand and somehow through the noise of Sanctum, I had heard his words.

He promised I would forget.

He promised I wouldn't even know he was gone.

He promised I wouldn't be sad anymore.

He promised I wouldn't miss him.

"Colby, I need help with this biology, please. My English is pretty good, but these words are killing me."

Why Malynn expected me to be good at biology was a whole other mystery.

"Give me a minute. I'll be right there," I shouted to her. Malynn had made a vow to Theo that she would stay with me for life. It was a good thing I liked the spitfire girl.

This morning, while still lying in the quiet, I had decided on a few things. Swallowing against the rising tears, I made a list.

1. Get my own apartment with Malynn.
2. Go back to school.
3. Stop thinking about Theo.
4. Stop dreaming about Theo.
5. Stop saying his name.

I stood up to go help Malynn when my heart began pounding. This was a normal event of late. Every time I thought about the events of the last couple of months, a panic attack would ensue.

"Shit, not again."

"I thought maybe my time away would

change you, but I see you're still the same foul-mouthed beauty you always were."

My feet failed me and I stumbled backward into my vanity, slamming my hand against the mirror and nearly breaking it.

The first thought that popped into my head was to run to him and jump into his arms—but then, I realized that if he was here, that I was pissed as hell at him for leaving.

In fact, I'd never been so completely furious with anyone in my life.

"Theo Ramsey, you son of a..."

But I couldn't possibly finish the sentence. Everything from the inside to the out of me was shaking from the trauma and from him being right in front of me.

"Are you real? Shit. I'm going nuts again, aren't I? I knew it."

He took one step toward me, and I scrambled to get away from him. If he touched me—or if he came any nearer and wasn't real, I couldn't handle it.

Either way, I couldn't handle Theo being back. If he was back, I would always be afraid he would leave again. And if he wasn't back, I wasn't sure I could ever go on with my life.

"I'm real, Querida. It's me, meu amada. Come here. Touch me."

I must've blinked a thousand times before my feet decided they were alive again. My chin quivered, the last standing part of me giving away my current mental status. It took me a full five minutes before I was standing in front of him. But he knew me well. He didn't make any motion to get closer.

I might've lost my shit if he had.

"How?" I asked before mentally chastising myself. I didn't give two pigs lips how.

"I don't know. I didn't really have time to ask. All I know was that the Almighty whispered to me as I was coming back 'It was not your time yet.'"

My eyes grew round. "And He just now decided? It took Him this long to decide?" My voice rose to yelling with each word.

He chuckled and patted his chest and abs like he forgot he had them. "Have you missed me at all?" Theo asked.

My first response was almost to slap him for such a ridiculous question. Every cell in my body missed him.

That was when the dam broke. There had been tears that had leaked and my fair share of crumbling walls, but with him here, everything I'd spent so much time holding together came tumbling down.

"Oh, Colby. I was trying to make you laugh. I'm sorry. I should leave the comedy to you."

I gasped when he grabbed my shoulders. With no gentleness, he pulled me against his rock-solid chest. His hands were in my hair, and he rained down an endless string of

Portuguese nonsense that at the time made all the sense in the world.

"You left me. How in the hell could you leave me? You promised. You promised I would forget you."

With his lips at my temple, he began to explain. "I know. I'm so sorry. You did forget for a while, I think. But there are some loves, Colby—there are some bonds that neither time, nor absence, nor distance can forget—and ours is one of them. When The Almighty fused us with the lightning, he did so for eternity. I was a fool to think it could be so lightly undone. I thought I was doing what was best for us—for you—for everyone."

I had been stiff in his arms, afraid that if I hugged him back, if I accepted that he was back, that he would be taken away from me again.

But when I remembered the lightning that had joined us—I knew he was right.

And I had no time to waste—we'd lost enough.

Pulling back from his chest, I fisted the collar of his white shirt and closed the distance between us. We crashed into a kiss that was long overdue—but never forgotten.

EPILOGUE
Collin

FOUR MONTHS LATER

NORMAL WOULD NEVER ENSUE AROUND THESE PEOPLE. They weren't normal to begin with.

Especially my mate.

I'd taken to clamping my lips together and shaking my head when Colby and Ari said something ridiculous—which was frequent.

But this was taking it too far.

"You want to get sealed where?"

Colby kidney-punched Ari. They also did that to me a lot, but I preferred it to the nut punching they were so fond of. Torrent could have all of that.

I groaned and grabbed at the beard Ari insisted I let grow out. "Why Kaskasapakte? I swear to the Almighty that if you say something about…"

"Because that's where your people are from, right? Don't tell me you are ashamed of your history."

I had learned that sometimes, it was just better to go along with them. They were a force to be reckoned with.

"Yes. That's where my people are from. Finally, I can admit it. I think it's a great idea. Let me braid my hair and line my eyes with the ashes of the dead. After I sharpen my axe and make vows to you in front of our friends, I will pillage and burn the people of the villages below us, making sure that if I die, I do so with honor to make sure I return to the glory of Valhalla."

Theo doubled over in the corner of our living room, laughing, with tears coming down his face.

Other than the sounds of his snorting, the place was silent. Finally, I had silenced the Smartass Twins.

It took Ari three rounds of opening and closing her mouth before she was able to say anything.

"Lining your eyes with the ashes of the dead? That is some serious guyliner. I'm not sure I want to know where you got that from."

She didn't? She was the one who made the entire neighborhood swear their silence every Thursday night when Vikings came on. She had the hots for Rollo.

It was something I put up with.

"Ari, please. Haven't you made the guy wait long enough? Let's just go to Hawaii, Fiji, Tonga, or something. You've got the dress. You've got the groom. You've got the—me."

Theo was not the Eidolon anymore. After being released from Paraiso, he no longer had the power to flash, walk through walls, or pinpoint Colby's location.

But to look at him and hear him speak, it wasn't obvious that he'd lost all of that power in one shot.

In fact, he was happier now than I'd ever seen him.

He held the same respect in our hearts that the Prophetess did and maybe even more. He gave up everything for our people. And we honored him for it by knowing who he was, but at the same time, treating him and Colby just like everyone else—except for times like this—when he was still allowed to officiate a sealing.

And he would be officiating our sealing.

Ari looked at me. From one second to the other, her face changed. It was the same face she made when a movie ended. But a little softer than the face she made when her lips tasted coffee in the morning.

It was the face she had in the morning light.

"I guess it doesn't matter, does it? It doesn't freaking matter. Who cares? Nobody. Theo? Can you seal us tomorrow in Belize? Belize is always good."

I didn't wait for Theo to answer. I walked over to Ari, lifted her by her waist, and crashed my mouth down against hers. She might be

high maintenance—she might have three times
the smart mouth that I did—but she was mine.

EPILOGUE 2
Colby

FIVE YEARS LATER

MALYNN HAD A BEATING COMING. IF SHE SHOWED ME that shit-eating grin one more time, I didn't care how big my belly was, she was going to get my foot shoved right up Main Street.

"Stop smiling at me like that. It's not funny."

Malynn lived in our guesthouse. Even though Theo had come back, she stayed true to her word. She was now my number-two best friend. At times like this one right here, where I had a two-year-old running around naked and a four-year-old who was currently painting the couch with shaving cream while I waddled the floor trying to rein it all in—she was kind of handy.

If she would only wipe that look off her face.

"This is not all. There are more to come. I told Theo that I saw it. Even when he was gone, the vision never changed."

What a know-it-all.

And if she talked to me about how many kids she had seen me having, I was going to

198

punch her in the uterus.

"Now, when I have a renter in the baby apartment and my bladder is the size of a flea's ass, is not the time to remind me of how many more tenants I'll be having in the future. So… either stop Theodore Jr. from painting with shaving cream or slap a diaper on Rebekkah. Either way, shut your trap and rustle up a kid."

She laughed but grumbled out something about grumpy pregnant women.

Grumble all you want, woman—just help.

"Colby?" she asked, choosing the naked kid.

"Yeah?"

"Do you ever think about that time? When things were different? Do you wish it had gone any other way?"

I thought about it all the time. When Theo came in from work in his suit and tie—he was now a website designer—I was reminded of the time when the world weighed on his shoulders and there was no clocking out for him—even during sleep. In between pregnancies, because I chose not to flash when I was pregnant, I went to some of the places we were during that time. Some of them conjured up good memories and some of them didn't.

Every time the kids called Uncle Torrent on Skype and I saw his face—it was hard on me still. I guessed that time would heal those things, but it was too soon, and I was too busy to even pay attention to it.

We didn't keep in touch with Regina or any of the other Synod. I assumed they went back to try to find some sense of normalcy. And while they had stepped in to help us fight a common enemy back then, I would never be able to forgive them for what they did to our people.

Sway and her mate put traveling bloggers to shame. They went everywhere—no place was off limits.

Collin and Ari had one son and named him Ramsey, after us. Ramsey and Rebekkah were born only weeks apart. Collin worked at the New York City library, but thanks to his flashing wife, he was able to live near us and work there at the same time. Thank goodness there were no security cameras in the basement of the library or else they would be in trouble.

We lived like anyone else.

We weren't afraid of being tormented anymore by shadows of so-called government people or conference tables full of women who threatened to take our powers. All of that was Sanctum and his cronies. He was taking our people's powers and blaming it on anyone he could.

He was the coward in the dark.

But we weren't afraid of the dark anymore.

"Querida, what mess are we in today?" He smiled when he got home, and I knew he was grateful for everything that had happened. We flashed together, of course, and I was grateful that I could bring my babies anywhere in the world that I wanted with the blink of an eye.

But sometimes, when Theo looked to the stars or outside in the rain, I saw the longing in his eyes. I knew the look so well.

The lightning, once it blew through temples and invaded veins, could never be forgotten.

"Not much. Rebekkah went to Columbia after turning on the TV. Damn Netflix and their National Geographic shows."

He chuckled and picked her up, whispering in her ear about not flashing without Mommy. He told them stories every night about how Daddy was once the Eidolon. He was their hero in those stories and every day.

"Mommy can bring us everywhere once she has your baby brother, okay? Or next time, you can bring me with you."

He brought her to the couch and sat down with her in his lap, and began a story about when we found out that we could travel together. She listened intently, hanging on every word, while I took the opportunity to sit and listen to his side of things.

I often think about the purpose of all those events, and I finally came to a conclusion: Everyone needed a wakeup call once in a while—societies where people were being treated inhumanely—countries where their children were starving—groups of people who used and abused others—and even the Lucents.

Even Rebekkah's death had a purpose. Five years later, the hate for what Sanctum did bubbles up and festers once in a while. We tolerate his presence, but things will never be okay between all of us.

We Lucents simply needed to be reminded that it wasn't a group of women, or scary people who chased us for our powers, that we needed to be afraid of.

All we needed to do was embrace who we were and be free—finally.

OTHER WORKS BY LILA FELIX:

The love and Skate Series:
Love and Skate
How It rolls
Down n derby
Caught in a jam
False start

Love and skate (the second Jam)

Bayou bear chronicles:
Burden
Hearten

Forced autonomy (a dystopian novella serial)

Anguish
heartbreaker
Seeking havok
Emerge
Perchance
hoax

Striking (co-authored by Rachel Higginson)

ACKNOWLEDGEMENTS:

I WOULDN'T BE HERE WITHOUT THE LORD GIVING ME A mind that likes to make up crap and tell everyone about it.

To my husband: If we could go anywhere in the world in a flash of lightning, I would still come home to you and our three stooges.

To Jaime Rodriguez, the best daggum PA in the world.

Rebecca Ethington, Ashleigh Russell, Mandy Anderson, Jamie Magee, and Delphina Miyares, thanks for sticking with me even when I sometimes push back.

To the Clean Teen Publishing Team: Rebecca, Marya, Courtney, and Melanie, y'all are the absolute best. I ask some pretty silly questions, but still, you answer with no hesitation. I am blessed to be a part of your team. Oh, Cynthia, bless your heart for having to put up with me. That's all I have to say.

Marya, you rock at the lightning. And the Theo. And the lightning making Theo even cuter. To all the bloggers who continue to support me, you rock. Keep up the amazing work.

There are readers, and then there are the Rink Rats. #RR4LIFE

About the Author

Lila Felix is full of antics and stories. She refused to go to Kindergarten after the teacher made her take a nap on the first day. She staged her first protest in middle school. She almost flunked out of her first semester at Pepperdine University because she was enthralled with their library and frequently was locked in. Now her husband and three children have to put up with her rebel nature in Louisiana where her days are filled with cypress trees, crawfish, and of course her books and writing. She writes about the ordinary rebels who fall extraordinarily in wild, true love. For more visit www.lilafelix.com

CPSIA information can be obtained
at www.ICGtesting.com
Printed in the USA
LVOW12s2042240716
497224LV00002B/10/P

9 781634 222051